Love at the Treble Clef Café

Veronika Sophia Robinson

Sweet Cinnamon Romance

For my beautiful daughters,
and our shared love of cooking.

Veronika Robinson is an Australian author living in rural Cumbria, England, with her husband, Paul, and two black cats, Kali and Pelé, in a three-hundred-year-old cottage overlooking the Pennines. As a teenager, she devoured romance novels instead of biology textbooks, and was regularly given detention by her science teacher for drawing "the wrong sort of hearts"!

In her mid twenties, after kissing too many frogs, Veronika met her soul's love, Paul. It was at this time that she became a marriage celebrant. All these years later, she still writes and officiates beautiful wedding ceremonies. Although voted by her secondary-school teachers as the student most likely to fail in life, Veronika couldn't be happier with the way she spends her days.

A late bloomer, in her mid fifties she earned her Master's Degree in Creative Writing from the University of Cumbria, despite no previous academic qualification. A prolific writer, her books span fiction and non-fiction.

Love at the Treble Clef Café
© Veronika Sophia Robinson
© Cover illustration by Heidi Harbers
Published by Sweet Cinnamon Romance
An imprint of Starflower Press
ISBN: 978-1-7398336-7-1

St. Valentine's Day 2023

A CIP catalogue record for this book is available from the British Library.

Published by Sweet Cinnamon Romance, an imprint of Starflower Press www.starflowerpress.com

Books by the same author at www.veronikarobinson.com

A Sweet Cinnamon Romance
will surprise you!

Burned

'Sequoia Lissen, you live such a charmed life!' Ali said to her best friend as she read through the letter. 'This is the second award that *Treble Clef* has received from the Tasmanian Tourism Board, and the café has only been opened for six months. How do you do it?'

'Perhaps I *am* charmed,' Sequoia smiled as she reached into the oven, wearing bright-yellow padded oven mitts. "Gorgeous," she said, as she breathed in the heavenly aroma of the freshly baked chocolate and stem-ginger cupcakes, sighing with pleasure and satisfaction. Careful not to burn herself, she placed the hot tray onto the wooden counter, continuing, 'Patrick's asked me out on a date, again. Since everything in my life is going so well, I might just say yes.'

'*Might* just say yes?' Ali swooped over to her and pretended to shake Sequoia's head. 'What's wrong with you girl? It's not every day that dashing young Belgian men come into this café and say they want to live the rest of their life with you. And he's promised that before even taking you on your first date!'

Sequoia attracted men like every you-can't-survive-her-charms cliché; but, for the most part, she was oblivious to their fascination. There had been a man in her life, once; and no other man was ever going to be good enough for her, so why bother? At least that's what she'd been telling herself for the past eight years.

'Yeah, well, we both know that he was probably exaggerating,' she said, her thoughts turning reluctantly back to Patrick. 'He's a natural flirt.'

Sequoia plucked each cupcake from the tray, humming a little as she placed them onto the cooling rack, proud that they'd turned out so perfectly. Then she headed back to the stove and stirred the soup, aware that the success of owning her first café had a positive impact on her whole being.

Sequoia reached over to Ali and retrieved the letter.

'These awards are lovely recognition, but they're not everything. It doesn't make *Treble Clef* a better café because we have them. It just means that someone took the time to notice what we do here, and nominated us. Come on, we open in ten minutes. Let's get the tables and chairs sorted.'

Ali looked on in bewilderment. 'How can you just shrug off prestigious awards and handsome men as if they came along every day?' Sequoia carried on with the jobs at hand, and the matter was closed, just like that. There was work to do, no time for celebrations or dancing a jig of triumph.

Sequoia climbed onto a high stool, and then wrote onto the large blackboard behind the counter.

Soup of the Day
Slow-roasted Red Capsicum
served with home-made sourdough rye bread

Chalk settled on her fingers, and as she sneezed in reaction to the white powdery dust, she heard a tap at the glass doors. It was Jack Breardon, owner of *Bay Books*, two shops down.

'Morning, Jack,' Sequoia said, welcoming him inside. 'Sure is a beautiful day. How are you?' She ushered him over to the counter, even though they both knew it wasn't officially open.

'Got some news, Sequoia. Not sure how to read it. This is just between us, okay? My mate, Heldon, on the council, says that new eco hotel next to the National Park...' he looked intently at the floor unsure of how much to share.

'What is it Jack? What's that development got to do with us?'

Jack was fifty years old, kind, divorced, and he'd had a soft spot for Sequoia from the first day he saw her: she was standing in the sunshine painting the front verandah of *Treble Clef* in sunflower yellow. With his long fingers, he brushed the blonde hair from his eyes, and Sequoia could see that he was troubled.

'S. Hazelwood Incorporated, that's the development firm; it wants to buy all the shops on the bay. We'd be answerable to a new landlord. Leases would change; rents would probably go up...' And again, he hung his head down as if surrendering to the inevitable. 'Word has it that this company can buy anything it wants.'

'But how does that affect us? They'd still have to charge market rate for the leases. I don't think it'll be a big deal, Jack...unless there's something you're not telling me?' For the first time, Sequoia felt her heart palpitate in a way that it hadn't done in years. Initially, she'd tried to ignore it, but the name Hazelwood made her feel like she was at the race track: a dozen horses' hooves pounding beneath her ribs. It wasn't like Hazelwood was a common name.

Eight years ago, she'd stepped onto Australia's largest island. Sequoia had come here in haste, to escape, to seek refuge; but from the second her feet landed on Tasmanian soil, she felt at home. Here, she was safe. No-one could harm her again. Ever.

For several years, she'd worked her way around the island, waitressing, baking, cooking: developing all the skills which led her to find the confidence to open her own café. *Treble Clef* was a hit not just with the locals of Coles Bay, but the tourists who drove up from Hobart, down from Launceston, or flew over from Melbourne and Sydney.

'What is it Jack?' she begged sensing he was holding back further information.

'Nothing I can put my finger on. It's just...It's just that I did my research on S. Hazelwood, and you know, there isn't anything which identifies who actually owns it. He has a first-class reputation for designing ecologically sound luxury five-star hotels, but this Hazelwood person is a recluse. And there isn't a single application for building permission that's ever been refused. I can't find out who S. Hazelwood is, despite his worldwide reputation. He's created hotels in just about every country around the world. Heldon says everything has been done through company lawyers.'

'So, they must be doing something right,' Sequoia said, trying to comfort Jack; but she was feeling edgy, as if she'd had three espressos too many.

'What's up, Jack?' Ali asked when she came back from placing vases on each table and caught them looking so serious.

'I'll fill you in,' Sequoia promised, as Jack walked away.

'He doesn't look happy!' Ali observed.

'Jack thinks there's trouble on the horizon. He might just be right,' Sequoia fretted; but there was no time to worry now as fifteen women from the Bay's Dancercise Class rolled up for their banana and cinnamon muffins and skinny lattes.

Ali served on the front counter, and Sequoia headed off to the kitchen to continue baking. The day had started so well, but now she was feeling jittery. It had only taken one word to set her on edge.

When Sequoia pulled out her menu list for the week, and spied hazelnut and maple cheesecake, her mind connected dots. Hazelnuts, she thought to herself. *Hazelwood.* It was too much of a coincidence. *Such an uncommon name.* She'd thought that eight years ago when he'd turned her fragile world right-side up, and then upside down again in the blink of an eye; and she was thinking it now. Forcing herself to take deep breaths, she said to herself 'Don't be silly girl. He doesn't know where you are.'

Sequoia set to work creating Jack's favourite cheesecake. Maybe it would cheer him up. She'd save a slice for him, and take it over later as a surprise. The morning was spent working at full pace fulfilling orders as soon as they came in.

Ali turned up with several lunchtime orders: avocado, tomato, and home-made hommous on stone-ground granary bread; cauliflower biryani with poppadoms; Greek eggplant and caper casserole with pasta; sweet-potato fries sprinkled with smoked paprika.

Sequoia didn't have time to think about long-lost loves, and mystery property developers. Her only thought was: *will I make it to 4pm closing time?* From time to time she'd stop and rub her legs where muscles ached. That, she could soothe, but her nerves were on edge. More than once she pounced on Ali to get the food to the customers more quickly.

'Crikey girl, what *is* your problem today?' Ali demanded when she finally shut the door to the last customers at 4.15. The upside to being best friends was that they could be honest with each other. 'You've been edgy and flighty since your conversation with Jack this morning. What's going on?'

Sequoia rubbed her eyes, and then stifled a yawn. 'I'm sorry. You didn't deserve me snapping at you. It's not you, it's me.'

There was only one person in Tasmania who knew why she'd come here, and why it had to remain a secret. Nervously biting her bottom lip, Sequoia said 'I think Ruben's in town.'

Ali instinctively reached out her hand to Sequoia's shoulder. 'Are you sure?'

'No, I'm not sure. Not sure at all.' She was hesitant. 'There's no way in the world he'd know where I am, and even if he did, there's no reason for him to come here. Maybe it's just coincidence. Maybe I'm short on sleep!' She tried laughing it off, but Ali knew better.

'What did Jack say?'

'That new five-star eco hotel near Freycinet National Park opening in a few weeks? It's been developed by S. Hazelwood Incorporated.'

'Oh honey, I know Hazelwood isn't a common name like Smith or Jones, but there must be hundreds of Hazelwoods in the world. Thousands, even.'

Ali tried to comfort her. 'And he's R. Hazelwood, not S.'

'He could have changed the initial so that he was recognised as a designer in his own right, rather than cashing in on the family name? He never felt comfortable with his identity being tied in with his family ancestry. It has to be him. A Hazelwood with that much money that they can buy out all the shops' titles in Coles Bay? And,' she chewed her bottom lip, 'Ruben had a degree in ecological architecture; and that's what this hotel is!' 'Oh,' Ali said, taking a step back. 'Oh.' She paused, and said, 'But I thought he was just like, you know, a rich fella's son?'

'Oh yes, he is that too! But underneath all the gold bullion, limousines, butlers, and castles sprinkled across Europe, was a heart with ethics. At least when it suited him!' Sequoia scowled. She didn't want to think about that side of him. The side that changed her world in a split second.

They were interrupted by a man knocking on the front door. Patrick Janssens stood there, smiling. Five feet eight, with dark, shoulder-length black curly hair, and shiny bright brown eyes, he waved to ensure he had Sequoia's attention. It was hard for the women not to melt. Everything about Patrick was charming.

'There's the lovesick puppy,' Ali laughed out loud, still in disbelief that a man could have such ridiculously long eyelashes without the addition of mascara. 'I'll leave you to him.' She grabbed her handbag and called back over her shoulder. 'I'll see you tomorrow.'

'See ya,' Sequoia smiled, but underneath, her heart was still pounding.

Ali let Patrick in the front door.

'Sequoia, don't refuse me,' he pleaded, dropping to his knees in a mock beg. 'Come for a walk on the beach with me. You've been cooking for everyone all day long, now you come with me and we eat a meal together.' Even his halting English was charming. How could she refuse him?

In a second, she slung her bag over her shoulders, and locked the door behind them.

'I've got wine. Let's head over there,' he said, 'to the far end of the bay.'

Don't fall too hard Patrick, she thought to herself. *I'm not free*. And it was true. To the whole world she was as free as a bird, but inside she still felt caged, somehow. Still in exile.

Patrick and Sequoia stopped by the fish and chip shop, and placed their order. Sequoia ordered a mushroom burger, chips, and battered pineapple rings.

'What?' she asked, when she saw him grin.

'You're so slim. How can you eat like that and not be overweight?' he asked good-humouredly; but she most certainly didn't find it a laughing matter.

'I'm hungry! I haven't eaten all day!' Sequoia felt defensive. It was true: she loved food. Good food, tasty food, plenty of food. Growing it, preparing it, sharing it, and eating it. But she also knew that to have a healthy appetite like hers meant having the same passion for exercise. It hadn't always been like that. When she and Ruben met, she'd carried about two stone more in weight. It had never bothered her, and Ruben loved her curves. All of them. More than once he described her voluptuous, feminine body as perfect. *Rubenesque*, he called her. And oh how he preferred her shape, he said many times, to the unhealthy-looking skeletal models who permeated his world. But the British Press tore her to pieces when photographers snapped pictures of them together at charity events. She'd been demonised as if she was morbidly obese, instead of the healthy and happy young woman that she was; and the media branded her as someone whose physical body brought shame to the Hazelwood empire. 'Dumpy Girlfriend' the headlines read. 'Send her to the Fat Farm!' 'One pie too many!' Sequoia had been traumatised. The agony of being hauled through the coal fires of the press had been a brutal taste of things to come.

'I'll eat what I want when I want!' she snapped. 'You're beautiful,' he offered, and tried to soothe a balm over the wound. 'No harm was meant. I'm sorry.' He was wise enough to know that whatever was bothering her was nothing to do with him.

Patrick had been flirting over the *Treble Clef* counter since the day it opened, and hanging around day after day, almost sloth-like. He'd been backpacking through the bay with two friends, and was drawn into the café by the smell of Sequoia's Hungarian mushroom goulash. After that, he never left. Within days, Patrick found himself a part-time job at the local sawmill. Every single day of business, he came by, often with Tasmanian wildflowers in his hand, asking Sequoia to go out with him: a walk, the movies, dinner, dance, and more than one offer of marriage. And always, she refused. *Tired,* she said. *Long day at work,* she said. Always an excuse at the ready. What she felt for him was affection, not attraction.

Though, she had to hand it to him: he was persistent. And, she admitted, he had grown on her. Patrick was 24 years old, three years younger than her. In some ways, he was more like fourteen, but on other days, when he was feeling particular protective of her, he acted like he was 44.

On the first night the café was ready for the dining public, Sequoia opened late with a candlelit supper. On the old grand piano in the corner, she played Hungarian dances; tapping out tunes till after midnight.

Patrick had been born and raised in the small Belgian town of Dinant, the home town of the saxophone. So when he turned up the next day proudly boasting his instrument, and asking permission to busk outside the café, she invited him in and they performed duets together. Patrick played sexy, sultry love songs on his golden saxophone, and Sequoia let her fingers dance upon the keys of the piano. If only she had the same spark for him as he held for her. They'd make such a great team. As time went on, she continued to see him as like a brother, much to Ali's annoyance.

By day, customers came in and tinkled the piano keys. Saturday was by far her favourite day, when the music-college students, lounging over lattes, improvised jazz pieces for hours on end. Customers spontaneously started dancing and singing. The free entertainment, and the fun nature of their music, drew crowds up from the beach.

'Patrick's lovely,' Ali said more than once, 'you should at least make an effort. Give him a chance!'

And so, that's what Sequoia was doing tonight, six months later: giving him a chance. But was she really? Was having a few chips on the beach with Patrick about him, or about running from Ruben and memories of the past? Was she really giving Patrick a chance when her heart had already been given away?

The evening was pleasant, and when Patrick walked Sequoia home to her little wooden cabin on the outskirts of Coles Bay, she let him hold her in his arms. Sequoia figured she had nothing to lose. After all, he was harmless. If there was anything she'd learned about Patrick Janssens in the past six months, it was this: he would never hurt her. Unlike *Ruben!*

Gently, and with some hesitation, he pulled her close to him letting his fingers brush over her pink cotton tunic, and onto her hands. Sequoia could feel his warm breath against her as he leant down to kiss her suntanned neck.

'You're precious to me,' he whispered.

Sequoia could feel the restrained urgency in his body: wanting her, fearful of overwhelming her, holding her close, holding her back, trying to read her cues, overwhelmed by confusion. Sequoia wasn't rejecting him, but she wasn't enticing him either.

'May I kiss you?' he asked.

'Yes Patrick, you may kiss me.' But no sooner had she agreed did she start wondering if it was a mistake. Wasn't this leading him on? Where was she leading him to? Certainly not to her bed! She had no intentions of letting it get that far. Ever.

It was the tenderness of his kiss that caught her by surprise. And she found herself quite enjoying it, but it didn't make her pulse race. Not like the way Ruben had made her feel. Ruben's kisses left her feeling as if someone was in hot pursuit.

It felt good to be held in someone's arms, she told herself, but was this the best she could expect to hope for from any man who wasn't Ruben Hazelwood? She wasn't sure, not sure at all, that she wanted to live a life of compromise.

The chill of Autumn made itself felt, and goosebumps pricked up on her arms.

Less restrained now, he responded to her encouragement.

'I want you Sequoia. I want you now.' And with those words, she found herself tumbling out of the bubble she was in, and back to reality. Back to her little kitten, Adagio, who was frantically circling her legs. She mewled at Sequoia's feet, demanding her evening meal.

'I'm sorry Patrick. Early start in the morning. Thank you for such a lovely evening.'

As her fingers fumbled, she finally managed

to unlock the front door, leaving him bewildered and rejected; his face as red as the riot of flowering geraniums bunched up in terracotta pots by her front door.

'I could stay the night,' he offered, hopefully, desperately.

Lovesick puppy. Ali was right about that!

'Thanks, but I really need to sleep.'

Sequoia feigned severe tiredness, and closed the door with Adagio scampering ahead.

Once inside, she fed the starving cat, then checked her answering machine messages.

"You have one message."

'Hi Sequoia. Jack Breardon. Did you get the gold-embossed invitation to all Coles Bay leaseholders? We're invited to a ball in the new hotel. Have you got a date? If not, would you do me the pleasure of letting me escort you?'

Invitation? Scanning her mind back through the day's events, she didn't recall seeing an invitation. And then she realised she'd not finished reading the business mail.

Sequoia tossed and turned all night. It was a disturbed sleep, filled with memories she tried in vain to erase. They tormented her, nipping at the heels of her history. Who was she? What made her the person everyone in Coles Bay loved?

The Invitation

Sequoia opened the cream-coloured envelope, her fingers shaking like the heartbeat of a hummingbird. *He has style*, she said to herself as the invitation opened in her hands. The paper was an exquisite parchment, and the hand-written calligraphy read:

Hazelwood Hotel
Invites you and a friend to the
Ball of the Bay
Coles Bay Road, Coles Bay, 7215
May 20th
6pm till late
Black tie

RSVP May 15th

Sequoia had never seen gold ink like it before, and then reminded herself that she lived in a different world to Ruben. Of course ink like this existed. It probably cost $500 a drop. Those old feelings of resentment towards the rich and wealthy came bubbling up like bile, reminding her that she was once part of that world, albeit briefly.

Ali snuck up behind Sequoia and read over her shoulder, then pulled it from her hands.

'So, are we going to this posh ball?' Ali asked excitedly as she waved the invitation around the café kitchen.

'Not really my thing Ali, you know that,' Sequoia replied sternly.

As far as she was concerned, she'd worn enough ball gowns to last a lifetime. She'd spent far too much of her time having designer dresses fitted on her, and her hair tended and teased by stylists. 'Nope, give me jeans and bare feet any day of the week!'

'Oh come on! It's just one night. I can even paint your toenails, and do your hair!'

Sequoia had to admit that her friend's enthusiasm was contagious. She hadn't painted her toenails in eight years, and she wasn't about to start now.

'You haven't even asked me about my date with the handsome puppy,' she smiled, changing the subject.

'Don't need to. Saw you kissing him on the doorstep, and then him walking away with hunched shoulders. Cruel, Sequoia. So very cruel.' Ali turned away so that Sequoia couldn't see the smile on her lips.

'Don't you even want to know what his kisses are like?' Sequoia teased.

'Can't be that good or he'd have walked through your door…'

'Actually, he kissed like a dream,' she fibbed. 'That's why I turned him away! I knew I wouldn't be able to say no. I'm a victim of my ovulating hormones!'

Ali responded: 'Really? I can't believe you have so much self-control,' she said in amazement. 'So, will you ask him to the Ball of the Bay?'

'Actually, Jack's already asked me if he can be my escort,' Sequoia said casually.

'He's old enough to be your father!' Ali squirmed in disgust.

'That may be true, but I don't see him as a father figure. I see Jack for what he is: kind, caring, gentle, humorous, wise, witty.'

'Oh please! Marry him already!' Ali interrupted.

'His heart isn't ready for marriage again. His body might be,' Sequoia giggled, 'but his heart isn't. I can tell a broken heart a mile away. Maybe one day. Oh, look at the time! We better get our skates on!'

They worked steadily on the day's menu, preparing soups, salads and chef's choices. Sequoia massaged shredded kale leaves with olive oil till they were limp and soft and all the raspy edges gone; she found herself thinking of Patrick's kisses, and then suddenly she was remembering how Ruben used to kiss her. She was *kale*. Weak as putty in his arms. Soft and yielding and giddy. Hard edges melting. At nineteen, she was powerless against his charms, and his warm smile.

Don't go back there, she told herself. *Don't go. You were little more than a girl. You didn't know any better!*

A few thin slices of red cabbage, toasted sunflower seeds, and freshly squeezed orange juice were added to the kale. This salad was always a favourite with the customers. Ruben's face was at the edges of her mind; memories of him in his fine dining suits, earthy cedar-and-sage aftershave, and limousine; his scent clinging to her heart like olive oil to kale.

Thoughts of Ruben and his penthouse suite in Paris, his villa in Tuscany, his houses in London, and castles dotted across Europe taunted her. They weren't all his properties; not yet, anyway. But he would inherit them at different ages of his life. Ruben Hazelwood was the only son of Fenton, and grandson of Lord Warwick.

Sequoia couldn't keep her mind on the job. Her heart was all aflutter. For eight years she'd done her best to exorcise every last Ruben memory. She'd fled Europe to protect her broken heart, and the humiliation he'd brought into her life. Sequoia most certainly did not need to go back down memory lane. Love, lust, and lies. What did she hope to remember?

'Just need to pop to the market and top up our

fresh-herb supply,' she said to Ali, as she prepared a cappuccino for a customer.

'See you soon, then.' Ali said.

Sequoia wasn't quite herself.

It's just a dance. She realised that Ali had no idea of how many dances Sequoia had been to, and how many times Ruben Hazelwood had swept her off her golden slippers.

Sequoia knew exactly what it was like to be the belle of the ball, and to have every man in the room undress you with his eyes and want to devour you, and leave you naked. She *knew*. But her heart had only ever been for Ruben.

Sequoia waved to Jack as she passed *Bay Books*, and appreciated the warm response. Who knows, she pondered, maybe one day they would take their friendship a step further? Jack ran out from behind the counter and caught up with her as she crossed the street.

'Did you get my answering-machine message?' he puffed as he arrived at her side.

'I'd love to go with you to the ball, Jack."

The evening dinner and dance would be a lovely opportunity for them to get to know each other a little better outside the confines of their work life. A chance for them to let their hair down, and relax.

'I'm just popping over to the Bay Market to get some produce,' she said.

'Mind if I join you? Annie's in the shop, so I can leave it for a few minutes.'

'Sure,' she smiled.

Sequoia picked out several bunches of fresh parsley, thyme, oregano, coriander and basil, and filled a few brown paper bags with sun-ripened cherry tomatoes. As she turned towards the salad leaves she was met by Jack carrying a beautiful bunch of pink lilies.

'Oh Jack,' she gasped. 'They're beautiful. Just beautiful. Thank you,' she whispered, breathing in their delicate scent.

'Beautiful flowers for a beautiful lady,' he smiled.

Sequoia raised herself on tiptoes to kiss him on the cheek, but as she did, her eyes caught sight of something wholly unexpected. A ghost, perhaps.

Looking right in her direction, a man of 6'3", in a black suit, dark-brown hair, deep-green penetrating eyes, and well-tanned skin, standing on the steps of The Bay's Barber, talking on his mobile phone. Their eyes locked. It wasn't the Ruben she remembered. No, this man had filled out a little more. More solid, more muscle, more *man*. It felt as if she lived a lifetime in those few seconds.

Electricity shot through her body, almost paralysing her, and she could see it had happened to him, too; he took a jolted step backwards. Feeling her face flush right down to her neck, she said to Jack, 'I need to get back to the café now.'

After she paid for the produce, Jack followed her across the street, and they went their separate ways.

'Thank you so much for the flowers. They really are ever so lovely,' she smiled; but inside her chest, her pounding heart was threatening to end her life. So, Ruben *was* in the bay? Damn.

'What's wrong with you?' Ali asked, almost under her breath so as not to bring attention from the diners. 'You look like you've seen a ghost!' She followed Sequoia anxiously to the kitchen. 'What's happened?'

There was only one word that she needed to say. One word that would illustrate that her life—her cosy, charmed, *perfect* life—was about to be turned upside down: '*Ruben!*'

'I still can't be one hundred percent sure, I mean, it's been eight years. Eight long years. Ali, he's grown into a man...I mean, a *man*. And no-one around here wears a suit like he was wearing. It would have cost more than some people's car! I can't breathe,' Sequoia said. 'I can hardly stand up.' Her flower-filled hand clasped at her chest. Ali passed her some water.

'What are you going to do? Do you think he saw you?'

Sequoia's face answered for her. She really didn't need to speak.

'Saw me? Yep. Just as I was giving Jack a peck on the cheek for buying me this beautiful bouquet,' she said weakly.

'Jack? Hope Ruben's not the jealous sort,' Ali grimaced.

'Oh he is. Well, he used to be. And,' Sequoia snapped 'what on earth can he be jealous of! He's married to someone else now. With luck,' she hesitated, 'maybe he didn't recognise me. I've lost a lot of weight since then, and my hair is a different style and colour.'

'Your eyes met, right?' Ali asked, wanting her suspicions confirmed.

'Met, locked...and yes,' she said, admitting defeat, 'recognised.'

'Crap.' And that's all Ali had to say. They both knew life was about to get really interesting.

Sequoia spent the rest of the day a jittery mess; cutting herself more than once, and burning her thumb on the gas flame.

'What am I going to do, Ali?' she asked for the twentieth time.

'You could track him down and ask what the hell he's doing here, or you could just get on with your life and pretend he doesn't exist.' The latter wasn't an option. Ruben had been Sequoia's first love. Sure, she'd only been nineteen years old, but there was no mistaking the depth of her feelings.

After work, Sequoia slipped off her shoes, and walked home along the beach, allowing the soft, cool sand to ooze between her toes. She willed her fears and anxiety to the waves. *Breathe, girl!* Sequoia nearly jumped out of her skin when hands wrapped around her slender waist.

'Patrick,' she gasped. 'You scared the life out of me!'

'I missed you,' he said calmly, sawdust clinging to his blue overalls. 'I missed you very much,' and turned her around so that he could kiss her. To her surprise, she succumbed. After the day she had, it was just the tonic. Soft, melting, warm.

Is it true that Belgian men are the best kissers in the world? She pondered this, and coming up for air, she tried to regain her senses.

'I really enjoyed last night, Patrick, but...' placing her hands firmly against his chest "but I need to take this slow. I'm really not ready for a relationship.' A few staccato blinks betrayed the hurt in his eyes. Sequoia didn't want to wound him, but she had to be honest.

'Six months, Sequoia. That's how long I've waited for you. I end my round-the-world travels, and I take a job at the sawmill. I wait for you at the end of each day. How more slow do you want?'

She intended to correct his English, but thought better of it.

Frowning, with her arms crossed in self-defence, she said 'Patrick, you really are the loveliest man, but I'm just not ready.'

'Let me help you be ready.' His lips persuaded her to stop arguing. Once again, he gently invited her into submission. Sequoia almost accepted. *Almost*.

'Patrick, please.' She didn't want to plead, and she knew he was too much of a gentleman to keep arguing.

'What do I can to change your mind?' He was fumbling over his words now. Lost for them; anxious to please.

'I need to go home. Adagio needs feeding, and I need to put my feet up. I'm sorry Patrick.'

'Goodnight beautiful lady. I keep waiting for you. I always keep waiting. To the last day on Earth, I keep waiting for you.' And he dropped to his knees, prayer-like, as she headed up the beach. What did she do to deserve such devotion? She shook her head in disbelief.

Carrying her shoes by the laces, and her handbag flung over her shoulder, she headed up to the roadside and let out a long breath, but she'd no sooner caught her breath than she stopped again. A large limousine was sprawled against the kerbside. Not that she could see inside the blackened windows, but she knew, just knew, that it wasn't a celebrity sitting inside watching her. It wasn't a celebrity watching her fall into Patrick's tender kisses. Damn.

Why did she care so much what Ruben Hazelwood thought? The man had made it abundantly clear that he didn't think much of her.

Sequoia dropped her head and averted her eyes so that if it was him inside he couldn't see her face. From her handbag she pulled out a pair of sunglasses. *Hopeless*, she thought, feeling so exposed. It was only half a mile to her little wooden cabin. Was it possible to get there without him seeing where she lived? Perhaps she should walk up another road, and disappear into the scrubland and put him off the trail? Yes, that's what she'd do. In an instant, she took the turn into the road by the creek, and then ran over the bridge and up through a thick belt of eucalyptus trees. Panting, she allowed herself a few minutes to steady her breathing. Why did she feel like she was on the run again? For years, that's what she'd done. Those days were supposed to be over! Sequoia's heart argued otherwise. Why run like a criminal, she'd done nothing wrong? What was she so afraid of? And why did she feel like Ruben was stalking her?

Before she made her way back onto the road in front of her house, Sequoia scanned the horizon. No black limousines in sight. Without hesitation, she ran up the steps onto the verandah and unlocked the door. Adagio was at her feet, mewling like there was no tomorrow. Sequoia locked the door behind herself, then allowed a few minutes to steady her nerves. Breathe girl, breathe.

The kitten demanded feeding, and then Sequoia showered. But perhaps that wasn't the best idea in the world: Hot steam and the sensuous feel of water against her breasts. How many showers had she shared with Ruben Hazelwood? *No*, she told herself. But it was too late. In her mind, his hands were over her, his lips touching hers, his body firm and hard against her tender flesh. *This has to stop!* Turning off the hot tap, she let icy splinters of water tame her treacherous body. Then, with a yelp of frustration, she grabbed a towel to dry herself.

After slipping into her nightdress, she decided it was best to have an early night. There'd been more stress in one day than she'd had in years. The red light flashing on the answering machine caught her eyes as she walked through the lounge room. Oh Patrick, she thought, please give up.

'Sequoia…' and just hearing him speak her name for the first time in eight years tore her heart apart. 'I suppose you thought I'd never find you?' The dulcet voice was unmistakeable. 'You can't hide from me now. Please let me see you.'

'Ruben!' She screamed, startling the kitten. With a voice soft as silk, even after all these years his honeyed mellifluous tone brought Sequoia to her knees. Powerless. Once again he cast a spell over her. He was right about one thing: there was nowhere for her to hide. Ruben knew that she couldn't just walk away from *Treble Clef*. That would be irresponsible. Nor could she walk away from her rental agreement on the house. Darn! Curse words were flung in the air; she couldn't walk away from the life she'd created here in the Bay.

This life of hers flashed before her eyes. All the choices she'd made: her carefully planned escape from Europe, away from the pain. Had it all been in vain?

Sequoia surveyed her small living area, simply decorated in a Moroccan theme with purple cushions and lanterns, and soft fabrics over the sofas. Unstained wooden floorboards, beeswax candles scented with jasmine, luscious house plants with an abundance of foliage, and other simple touches that calmed her, filled her humble but well-loved home. This was the life she'd handcrafted for herself; the life she loved. Was Ruben Hazelwood about to pull it all apart, thread by thread? The only thing she knew to do was to stay strong. She'd done so before, she could do it again. *I'm not for sale!* she yelled. If there was anything she knew for sure about the Hazelwoods, it was that, for them, everyone had a price.

It was that dark hour, just before sunrise, when she finally fell asleep on the lavender-coloured linen sofa, exhausted and tormented. Fitful sleep, haunted dreams, and not-quite-extinct memories of passionate and explosive love-making swirled in like the Autumn fog at the corners of her mind. Adagio lay in her lap, purring. And those contented sounds reminded Sequoia of when she too felt like that: warm, content, happy with life. Purring made her think of a time when she felt like the most-loved woman in the world.

The violent buzzing of the phone startled her, and rudely brought her back to reality; she was not loved by Ruben Hazelwood, and she was not content. Not any more.

'Hello?' she asked wearily into the phone.

'*Treble Clef* opened an hour ago! Where the hell are you?' Ali demanded.

'Oh Ali…Give me twenty minutes. I'll be there as soon as I can.' She dropped the phone into its cradle, and dressed quickly in jeans, and a pretty pink-and-mandarin-coloured floral blouse, fuchsia-tinted crocheted cardigan and pink sandshoes. If there was one thing guaranteed to stress her, it was dressing under pressure, and arriving at work in a frazzled state. Sequoia rarely slept in.

Adagio insisted on breakfast, and then Sequoia was out the door, bunching her dark-brown hair up into a loose bun, and watching for black limos and tall handsome men. There were neither, and she felt herself breathing more easily.

'I'll explain later,' she muttered when she swung by Ali at the front counter. As she entered the kitchen, she surveyed the scene: it looked like a bomb site. Running *Treble Clef* was not a job for the faint-hearted, nor for one person. Sequoia didn't know where to start: dishes or food prep? She caught the simmering wild-mushroom soup just before it stuck to the bottom of the pan. Sequoia witheld a scream. While she adored the buzz of café life, she did not like filthy dishes from wall to wall or chaos in her kitchen. And that was why Ali worked out the front on the counter and Sequoia was in charge of the food in the kitchen!

Methodically, and with gritted teeth, she worked her way from one end to the other, creating structure from mess. Within half an hour, her workspace was back in order, and she was calmly preparing lunchtime meals: eggplant curry; ratatouille; Chinese-style fried rice; ploughman's sandwiches filled with local organic cheese and topped with Sequoia's homemade spicy apple and sultana chutney, and fresh salad vegetables.

'You never sleep in,' Ali said as she shut the front door at 4.20pm. 'What's going on? This Ruben has really spooked you, I know that but what's with the sleep-in?'

Sequoia explained the lingering kiss on the beach with Patrick, and the limo, and the race home, and the message from Ruben on the answering machine.

'Oh boy. There's nowhere to run now, girl; you're going to have to face the music.'

'I just hate feeling like I did something wrong. It wasn't me who just up and left and got married! The only thing I did was leave Europe and start my life afresh; free of him and all the memories. Why do I feel like the criminal here?'

Ali shook her head, completely at a loss as to how she could best support her friend.

'Just take one day at a time. That's all you can do anyway, right? I guess he'll be gone when the new hotel is underway and running efficiently. Look, I need to go home. Matt is finishing early so we can go out and watch the new Russell Crowe movie. See you tomorrow? Don't sleep in!' she smiled, trying to offer some semblance of comfort.

Sequoia locked the front door behind Ali, and settled herself at the baby grand. It was the piano which had brought such comfort into her life, and she realised she needed to play, if just for an hour or so. It would help her unwind. And so she began, doing what she always did: playing her composers in alphabetical order, just as if she was filing away herbs and spices neatly. Beauty and order. Bach, Beethoven, Brahms, Chaminade, Chopin, Debussy, Mozart, Rachmaninoff, Saint-Saens, Schuman and Tchaikovsky. *Calm*. Ah, that's better.

An hour later, as the sun set over the bay, she was unware that a tall figure eased up beside the front door of *Treble Clef*, listening to the sounds of the piano. Ruben was close to her now. So close, and yet so far! Nor did she hear a tortured moan escaped his lips; his pain muffled by the piano music. How was Sequoia to know that the melodies returned him to that stormy night, eight years ago? That night, when Sequoia entered his heart and unravelled everything he'd ever been taught.

The Way to a Man's Heart

Lightning struck, briefly illuminating the tiny French village. The only light on in the main street was above a small traditional bakery; an old stone building some three hundred years old. The village was all but asleep at just after midnight.

Ruben stepped out of his BMW, dodging the sharp pellets of rain, and knocked on the front door of the *Artisan Boulangerie*. For twenty minutes he tried to get the attention of whoever was upstairs, but his knocks couldn't be heard above the piano playing and rumbles of thunder. The music mesmerised him. In no time at all, he'd forgotten that he was lost, or how inhospitable the Spring storm was, and his need for directions was replaced by an obsession to meet the pianist: to have them come and play for him. After a while, he gave up and waited out the night in his car. It was a long evening, but his discomfort was eased by memories of beautiful music.

At first light, he awoke to find the village was in a leafy valley near a winding river, and was immediately charmed by the romantic sight of its steeply roofed houses, clustered melodiously around the Romanesque church and the castle.

'Happy 25th birthday, Ruben!' he chuckled to himself. The irony: Sitting in his crumpled Caraceni business suit, after a night in the driver's seat of his black convertible, and he was actually happy. Happy for the first time in such a long time. No doubt his father would have been ashamed at the state of him. Ruben could hear his condemning voice all the way to France. *Disgraceful!*

A figure in the bakery was making preparations for the day. Medium height, almost tall, with her hair tied up in a tight bun and a few wispy strands of hair settling over her high cheekbones, Ruben was transfixed by how the dim lights inside highlighted her silhouette. The vision of beauty before Ruben made him grateful that his satellite navigation had broken, causing him to lose his way back to Paris the night before.

After several firm knocks on the front door, he was met by the young woman. No longer a silhouette, but real. Oh yes, she was real.

'We're not open for another hour, sir' she said politely, first in French and then in English.

Ruben found himself tongue-tied, and he wanted to wipe the single tear in the crescent of her eye.

'I lost my way, and needed directions. I knocked last night, but couldn't be heard above the storm and ... was it you playing the piano?' he asked.

'Yes, sir. Where are you heading?' Sequoia asked, wanting to avoid the intrusion into her personal life.

'Paris. I seemed to have ended up on the wrong road, and can't find my way back to the autostrade.'

Sequoia drew directions onto a piece of paper, then wished him well.

'Have a lovely day,' she said softly, averting her eyes, then proceeded to dress the front window with fresh loaves, small hessian bags filled with wheat, and bunches of lavender.

Ruben had no intention of going anywhere. Enchanted by her raw beauty, there was something self-sufficient about her, and she certainly didn't bow down at his feet like every other woman in his life did. It was oddly refreshing, he decided, if not somewhat disconcerting. This was unknown territory, in every

31

sense of the word. Feeling bold, he invited her to play for him at a charity event for Romanian orphans.

'Thank you sir, but I don't play in public. I play privately, and never to an audience.' She was firm, but polite, and even accorded him a sweet smile.

Ruben couldn't help notice her flush as she avoided eye contact. He wasn't to know that devastatingly handsome men like him never came to her village, and that he'd taken her quite by surprise. How could he possibly know that she was inwardly reprimanding herself for thoughts like: *he'd never be interested in a girl like me!*

Ruben was taken by her beautifully spoken voice, and couldn't quite place her accent. She wasn't French, that was clear, or so he thought, though she had a hint of it in her vowels, but she also seemed to have a little American twang tucked up with well-spoken English, and perhaps a bit of...no, he couldn't work it out. Australian? No. Maybe. Well-travelled, perhaps, is what he decided. Ruben had traversed the world countless times, for business and pleasure, and had never heard an accent quite like it. He found it simply added to her charm — and it made him smile that she couldn't be put in a box. It intrigued him, and taunted his well-structured existence. Nothing, not a single thing, in his education had prepared him for her. Simply by being herself, she was a threat to everything he'd ever learnt.

Not one to give up, he tried again. 'These are poor homeless children without loving families. You won't play to raise money? I can pay you whatever you like, and then we could raise even more money for them.'

'Guilt will get you nowhere, sir. Instead of paying me, why don't you just give your hard-earned money straight to the children? If you care that much? Cut out the middle girl.' She defiantly raised her left eyebrow as if to mock him. He was taken aback as she nearly choked on the words *hard-earned*. She probably thinks I've never done a day's work in my life, he mused as he caught sight of his perfectly immaculate hands. If he didn't know better, he was sure the look on her face was contempt. Oddly, he felt admiration for her stance. No-one in his whole life had ever rejected him before. What was she, seventeen, maybe eighteen? And despite her shyness, was stronger than any woman he'd ever met. Oh how he loved her feistiness, and wanted to cling on to every word she said, only to replay each one over and over.

For a while, he stood leaning against the front counter watching her work. It was clear she'd been awake for some time already, baking. Ruben studied her as she carefully placed several baskets on an old, oak table.

The baskets featured her early-morning creations: pains de Campagne, pains au Levain, mushroom fougasse, herb roulé and poppy-seed baguettes. On the front counter, she offered a selection of items for the patisserie: coffee éclairs, almond croissants and apple chaussons. Ruben was close to her now, breathing her in: trying to draw her close to him in any way that he could. The scent of cinnamon, apple and sultanas clung to her hair.

'Would you play for me, then? Just me,' he asked quietly.

Sequoia looked up from the loaves of bread she was handling, and he felt her study his face for a few seconds. And that's when he knew for sure: she found him attractive. Her skin had become slightly mottled with shades of pink.

'That, sir, would be playing for an audience. No. Now, can I get you any bread or pastries, sir?' she asked politely, and using a long-handled, hand-carved wooden paddle, she reached into the back of the wood-fired brick oven. Although her back was now to him while she removed several loaves of sourdough rye bread, Ruben knew that she was waiting for him to decide what he wanted. When she turned around, he noticed that she was surprised he was still in her boulangerie, Ruben watched the tears swelling in her eyes again.

'Why are you so sad?' he asked kindly; and his tenderness caught them both off guard. As her strong walls of defence came crashing down around her loaves of stone-ground bread, Ruben was desperate to hold her.

'I lied, sir.' She gratefully accepted the clean handkerchief he proffered.

'*Please* stop calling me sir.'

'Forgive me, but how am I supposed to address a man such as yourself?'

'Ruben. My name's Ruben.' It was all he could do not to wrap his arms around her, and protect her from whatever was troubling her.

Ruben absorbed the words behind her sadness.

'I lied. I *was* playing to an audience last night. My mother.'

'My mother is dying, and she gains great comfort from my playing.' And that was all she had to say.

Ruben's listened to the sound of her rapid breathing, then marched behind the counter, and put his arms around her. No sooner had he pulled her close, did she sob into his strong chest; and he held her, while she let go of the loss, the ache. And in that instant, he fell in love with her: right there, that morning, with flour dusted on her apron and her nose, surrounded by old jam jars filled with colourful wildflowers, and the heavenly aroma of freshly baked bread.

For the next few weeks, Ruben drove down each night from Paris and sat outside the boulangerie, with the roof of his car down, and listened. Memorising each tune, he took in the sound of every note. Ruben would be patient. Any day now, Sequoia would need him. And he knew that she wouldn't turn him away in her greatest hour of need.

Ruben Hazelwood came from a long line of men who taught him that everyone has a price. But Ruben was beginning to wonder if that was true for the unusual young woman in the boulangerie. Perhaps his father and grandfather had been wrong? After all, they'd never met the beautiful Sequoia Lissen. More woman than girl, but still with an innocent light in her young eyes.

Each morning he entered the boulangerie hours before it opened, worn out from sleeping fitfully in his car, and bought several loaves of bread. They both realised it was a cover so that he could visit her, and that he wouldn't miss the twenty euros he spent there each day. There were times when he wasn't sure whether she was cross that he'd never actually eat most of the bread or pastries, or pleased that he'd gone to so much effort.

Each day, Ruben learnt more about Sequoia.

'My mother is French, and was raised in an English boarding school,' she told him one sunny Spring morning. 'My French grandfather had owned

35

the boulangerie. It had been in his family for three generations. I lived the first five years of my life in California.'

Each morning, Ruben watched in admiration as she blind-baked dough, or retarded the yeast or stacked brioche moulds into the oak cupboard.

Before he knew it, Sequoia became an essential part of Ruben's every day life. And it delighted him that there was a sparkle in her eyes when she opened the door each morning. Despite her underlying sadness, he found that she was laughing more than crying. Not once did he let on that he slept outside the boulangerie every night, listening to her play or how much he looked forward to hers being the first face he saw each day.

Ruben had never worked so hard in his life; that was true. Winning her trust and affection was a slow process. But now that his studies in ecological architecture were over, he had all the time in the world.

When he arrived late on a Tuesday night, and heard nothing but the story within the silence, he knew: Sequoia's audience had gone, and she had no one to play for.

Ruben was desperate to hold her, to tell her everything would be okay. That he'd look after her. That she could play for him. How could he reach her? There was no answer to his frantic knocks on the door. Nothing worked: yelling; beeping his car horn; circling the building round and round.

The next morning, the doors of the Artisan Boulangerie remained firmly closed.

Ruben panicked. How could he be there for her, to comfort her, if she didn't let him in? Ruben sought out the parish priest, and made plans to be at Sequoia's mother's funeral in two days time.

Several extravagant bouquets were delivered to her home, and to the church for the funeral. There were white roses, Casablanca lilies, Lily of the valley, peonies and rare orchids. He signed them simply: *'Love, R. x'*

On the day of the funeral, the beautiful floral displays and arrangements adorned the village church. Ruben caught the small smile that had settled onto her face. It was as if he could read her mind: *He is thinking of me.*

It was a simple church service, with the burial in the churchyard.

Ruben stood, inconspicuously, in the shade of the oak trees at the edge of the cemetery. Despite Sequoia being shrouded in grief, Ruben could feel her gratitude for the flowers and his presence. Finally, he made his way from the back of the congregation to the front, closing the gap between them. Together. They were together now. Ruben held her for at least ten minutes as she sobbed into his beautiful made-to-measure Attolini suit until they were interrupted by the priest.

'Sequoia, everyone is going to the hall now. Will you and your friend join us now?'

Ruben and Sequoia walked hand in hand, and in a daze the afternoon ticked by, slowly, ever so slowly, as people paid their condolences. But not once did Ruben let go of her hand, even when people reached over to hug Sequoia. He wasn't letting her go. Not now. Not when he'd already waited far too long.

They were from such different worlds; he knew that the first time they met. Why was he so interested in her? He wondered. *She's barely an adult, working in her mother's simple boulangerie. I am from a world where money can buy everything. A world where I can have any woman I want.*

Sequoia was clear that no matter how darn gorgeous he was, or how attentive to her grief-stricken needs he continued to be, she was not going be a notch on his bedpost. She'd make sure of that! No man was going to take advantage of her loneliness and vulnerability. And she was lonely. Desperately so. Her mother had been a constant companion for nineteen years, and now Sequoia was alone. As a child, she'd been homeschooled in the pretty, yet remote, village; and spent her days playing the piano, and learning to bake bread and pastries. Everything was different now. Bleak, somehow. Her mother had brought warmth and joy to her life, and her death had taken that away.

No, she decided, she was not going to get involved with him.

Ruben, she soon realised, had other plans. Each day after the funeral, he drove down from Paris into the small village that was Sequoia's home. It had fewer than two-hundred residents. Ruben asked how anyone could sustain a thriving business here. It defied logic! The centre of the village was small, and there were just enough residents and stray tourists to eke out a living.

One morning, when she came downstairs at four, Sequoia was surprised to find that Ruben wasn't parked out the front of the boulangerie No car, no Ruben. Maybe he'd finally given up? And with that thought, her heart jolted. Perhaps she'd become more dependent on him than she'd realised.

There was little time to mourn. Life continued, and each day she baked loaves of sourdough rye bread, croissants, quiches and wholegrain rolls. Passing trade would come from lost tourists. It usually did. Sequoia smiled, grateful to the hooligans who'd torn down the road sign at the river junction, and even more grateful that it had never been replaced. It had increased traffic to their little business. And how different her heart might feel if Ruben hadn't got lost in the thunderstorm that night? Fate. Destiny. And there it was: *she was in love*. It had taken her all these months to see what was staring her in the face, and now it was too late!

With a heavy heart, Sequoia swept the floor, then opened the front door ready for business hours.

There, on the doorstep, was a parcel and envelope. Intrigued, she opened the parcel first, and inside she found a hand-bound copy of some of Mozart's handwritten manuscripts. Sequoia could barely keep herself standing upright. She had to sit down. Her legs were wobbling, and her fingers shaking. How much did this cost? Ruben did this for *me*? Ruben cares that much for me that he sourced this rare and priceless gift? Almost too scared to hold it, she let it rest against her chest. Tears slid from her eyes, and splashed down onto the letter in her hand. Sure he could afford anything he wanted, she figured, but to actually go to the effort of finding this? Sequoia marvelled at his neat handwriting, and wondered what it said about him. Each stroke, in fountain pen, was neat and clear. Her fingertips traced his words.

'Come to my place, play for me. No money. No charity. No guests. Just me. Play for me. Just a few tunes, and we can have a bite to eat. Please?
Pick you up at 7pm. Love, Ruben x'

'The arrogance!' but Sequoia couldn't help laugh. Giddy at the thought of seeing him again, she realised how much she'd missed his smile this morning. By 7pm, Sequoia was dressed in jeans and a lime-green chiffon blouse with lavender flowers embroidered at the hem and at the cuffs of the three-quarter-length sleeves. She sprayed wild-rose deodorant under her arms and on her pulse points. Looking out of the window, she saw a hint of the black car, and hurried down.

As she stepped out onto the street, she realised it wasn't his BMW, but a limousine. The chauffeur opened the back door, and ushered her in while introducing himself as François.

'Underdressed, right?' she asked, feeling somewhat embarrassed. Of course I shouldn't have worn jeans! What *was* she thinking!

'He won't mind dear. He's not like that all,' the elderly man assured her. 'Don't give it another thought.'

They drove in silence for a little while, and then he said, 'I've been enjoying your baking very much, you know. He must be keeping you in business with the number of loaves and pastries he buys.' The driver chuckled quietly at the lengths Ruben was going to in order to woo this young lady.

'At least he's not throwing it away,' she replied, relieved that her baking was feeding such a lovely man.

An hour later, dazzled by the night lights of Paris, Sequoia reflected that it had been quite some time since she'd been in the city. She preferred rural life—it was way less complicated. Despite this, she admired the night life of Paris, with its world-famous buildings, and the architecture lining wide avenues. It sparkled with sophistication beneath its bright lights.

Sequoia felt a shiver of anticipation and excitement. What was she expecting to happen tonight? She wondered. Ruben simply wanted her to play the piano, nothing more.

She checked her thoughts, and put them in place.

The driver slowed down at the traffic lights, by the old buildings on the side of the river Seine. Sequoia wound down the window and breathed in Paris: elegance, history, culture and style. She'd come here a couple of times each year with her mother to take in shows, and eat in fancy restaurants.

In front of the hotel where Ruben lived, Sequoia was taken aback by the parade of doormen, and waiters hovering like penguins inside the café on the ground level. The large glass windows invited the outdoors in.

'Have a lovely evening,' the driver winked.

'I hope I do,' Sequoia said shyly, realising she was rather nervous.

Once she'd stepped out of the vehicle, she quickly observed that she was completely out of her comfort zone. Surveying her jeans and sneakers, Sequoia summed it all up in one word: darn. For a moment, she hoped he wouldn't mock her ambivalent attitude to a night in Paris.

When Ruben opened the door of his penthouse suite, he'd barely said hello; had scarcely a chance to take her in: the way she smelled, like Summer peaches and evening rain; how her beautiful chocolate-coloured hair cascaded around her shoulders, and that her dark-brown eyes were like deep pools, and the easy way she carried her curves with grace. No, he'd barely had a chance to savour her at all before she spoke.

'I don't like this!' she said, striding right into the main room as if she owned the place, and throwing her hands high above her. 'I thought I was coming to play the piano and have a bite to eat?' She stormed around the room, and indignantly raised her hands again in protest over the romantic table for two. It was lined with several fine-silver forks, knives, spoons, linen napkins, and candelabras.

'It's a way of life. This is what I've grown up with. They're trappings. They make life easier but they're not who I really am. Look past them, Sequoia. See me. See *me*,' he pleaded. But Ruben doubted that she'd heard a single word of what he said. With her back to him, she was at the large glass windows taking in the view of Paris at night. Sequoia was mesmerised at what money could buy.

'Yes, I have endless advantages, but I've spent years working out who I am, and finding my place in the world; trying to find an identity that doesn't include my ancestry. Believe it or not, I want to be known for more than just being a rich man's son!'

Despite her protests and gruff entrance, their conversation was easy. When Sequoia ended up eating with her fingers, she noticed Ruben simply followed her cue. Before too long, she made herself at home in his opulent world. Of one thing she was absolutely certain: Sequoia was sure of who she was, and delighted in the way his expressions changed depending on what she was doing or saying: how her laughter pulled at him, or the way she flicked her hair whenever she was about to speak. It soon became apparent to her, that she made him feel a bit unsure of himself.

Ruben found Sequoia captivating and gorgeous. For a young nineteen-year-old woman, who was used to working hard and destined for a life of early mornings and manual labour, she looked right at home on his 10,000 euro sofa, her bare feet tucked up beneath her. Ruben wondered if she'd painted her toenails especially. She didn't strike him as a nail polish sort of girl. No, not at all, he decided. Willing to wager that she'd never painted her toenails before in her whole life, it made him smile that, despite wearing jeans, she'd made an effort.

Sequoia played the piano for three hours, and whenever she wanted to stop, Ruben would say 'one more'. Each time, she gave in. Ruben could tell she'd fallen just as deeply as he had, and he wondered what tomorrow would bring.

'I have to go home,' she said at one o'clock. 'I have a four am start. That bread won't bake itself!'

Ruben sighed, and gently invited her into his arms. And that was the end of everything she ever knew. Life would never, could never, be the same again. This was the moment they'd both waited their whole lives for, but until this moment they'd had no idea. Ruben held her close, his warm breath against her cheek. Should he kiss her? Surely he would; but then, instead, he just hugged her tighter.

'Please kiss me,' she asked, barely more than a whisper.

'Did you really think you were going to get away from me that easily?' Without waiting for her answer, Ruben swooped down, his firm mouth meeting her fuchsia-pink, lip-glossed soft lips, and together they fell into the quicksands of pleasure, and consumed by time itself. With hungry kisses that started so urgently, with no time to waste, Ruben realised she wasn't going to run away; he slowed down — so, so slowly now — each kiss one of succulent tenderness.

Aware that her knees were going to give way, Ruben carried her to his bed.

'I have to go home, I have to bake...' she pleaded, but he pretended time didn't exist for them. Ruben straddled above her, and undid the buttons of her blouse, sighing deeply when he revealed her soft and tender skin.

'I'll drive you home, and you'll be there for four. I promise.' But he couldn't keep talking. 'Right now, you're driving me....driving me *crazy*.'

Words turned to gravelly groans as he reached towards her yielding and ample breasts. They met him, and her erect nipples told him everything that her words couldn't: *I'll stay with you Ruben. Make love with me.*

'I need to be back for four,' she whispered, her face turning away from his.

'You've never done this before?' Ruben sighed in disbelief, and fell onto his back on the bed, exasperated. Of course she hadn't! 'Why didn't you tell me?' he asked, his face mired in frustration.

Dismayed, Sequoia protested 'You never asked!' Covering the shirt over her breasts, she demanded 'Is that it? I'm a virgin, so you just stop?'

Ruben was taken aback by her feistiness, and settled her down before kissing her forehead.

'It's a huge responsibility to make love with a woman for the first time. To take that from her.'

'It's a huge responsibility *every* time you make love with a woman!' As Sequoia stood up, and prepared to leave, he caught her by the hand.

'Not so fast!'

Slowly, he undressed her, and as every minute passed he recognised that she was more woman than anyone he'd ever been with before. In many ways, he thought, it was he who was unskilled in the art of lovemaking despite years of practice. As Sequoia lay naked against the silk sheets, Ruben delighted in each kiss.

It seemed to Ruben that Sequoia was in tune with her sensuality and femininity, and responded instinctively to his every touch, like a candle being lit, and lighting up the dark. Ruben held her gently, caressing each rhythmic rise and fall, as she just crossed the threshold of intimacy. There was no going back. Not ever.

They couldn't have been asleep for more than an hour when he woke Sequoia with his kisses.

'Come on, my love. It's time to wake up.' At the first hint of dawn, he gently coaxed her with his strong, hard body against her pliant soft curves, inviting her into his warm, soft kisses.

They drove back to her home in silence; a comfortable silence that offered a brief cushion to the impending separation. Words weren't necessary. They left each other to their memories of the beautiful night they'd shared.

As Ruben pulled up in front of the boulangerie, he said 'I have to head back to England. May I see you again before I leave? Or,' he hesitated, 'perhaps you could come with me?'

'That's not possible. I have the bakery to run. Thank you, though.'

He didn't want to spend a day apart from Sequoia. Not now. Not ever. She was under his skin like a powerful narcotic.

'I could cover your costs. Why not take a month or so off?' Ruben cringed at the desperation in his voice, and tried not to beg.

'That's very kind, but it's not just about the loss of earnings. It's about responsibility. The people in this village rely on daily fresh bread. Many people come in

45

twice a day. It's our tradition.'

'What if I employed a replacement baker for you? I could employ the best baker in France, if that's what it would take. Would you come with me then?'

It was clear that he'd do anything for them to be together.

'Really? You'd do that?'

'I would do anything for you Sequoia. Anything at all.'

Ruben walked away from the front door of *Treble Clef*, and left his pianist playing into the dark night. He had time. His beautiful memories would sustain him for however long it would take to win her back. And he *would* win her back, no matter what it cost him. After all, he was a Hazelwood.

A little while later, when Sequoia finished playing she sighed as she pulled down the lid over the piano keys. In her mind, she'd been playing for Ruben. Only Ruben. Just like she did on their first night together in Paris. And when she thought about what happened afterwards, a shiver rushed up her spine.

Menu Choices

At dawn, Sequoia was breaking lettuce leaves for the large leafy-green salad she prepared at the café every morning. With each tear of a tender green leaf, she felt her own heart ripping: Patrick, Jack and *Ruben!* She hissed at herself. *Don't be stupid, Ruben's married. And you haven't spent the past eight years detoxing him from your system just to have him come and take over your every waking thought again.* She focused her mind, and thought of each man individually, rather than as a trio she was forced to choose from.

Patrick was sweet. There was no denying that. He adored her, and made it clear that he was as lovesick as was possible: he'd sit on the café verandah for hours, ordering coffee after coffee, just so he could have the odd snatched moment with her; taking in her chocolate-coloured eyes, which sat like dark pools above her high, sculpted cheek bones. Just a minute with her radiant smile, and easy dimple; that's all he wanted, he had said to her. Sequoia knew it wouldn't satisfy him for much longer. Patrick's wish was to have her for hours, days, weeks, months, and yes, years. Life would have been simpler if she felt the same about him. And then she wondered, perhaps she didn't need to. Maybe, with time, she'd fall in love with him? After all, she'd been in love before, and look how that turned out! No, perhaps she should give him more of a chance. Maybe, she decided, she didn't need to hold her heart so rigidly in her chest.

Oh Jack, she thought, *lovely Jack,* as his face came into her mind. Not for a moment did she care about their age difference. What she saw was a man who'd been hurt in love, and who'd never hurt her. A man who would hold her tenderly, and love her into old age. Isn't that what we all wish for, she wondered, to love forever, rather than just in the first heated flush? For someone to know us better than we know ourselves?

Sequoia grabbed a handful of baby spinach leaves, rocket and basil, and ripped them into the large stainless steel bowl. Rip! There went her heart again. What direction should she go? What choice should she make?

Oh Ruben! Why did you have to break my heart? Why wasn't life easier than this? Memories of Ruben's wedding photos, splashed on the front of all the main British newspapers, and some of the French ones, filled her mind. She thought of how the residents of her little French village had gathered around her, and tried to put her back together again. But Little Miss Humpty Dumpty, well, she was broken! Well and truly broken, and all the village people, and the kind and honest priest, they couldn't put her back together again. Her heart splattered across the pavement that morning, like uncontained bright-yellow yolk, for the whole world to see. That one unforgettable morning; the one which changed her life forever. Whatever Ruben was doing in Coles Bay, it had nothing, nothing whatsoever, to do with her. Sequoia was one hundred per-cent sure of that.

It was his daily morning latte that brought Jack into her café at 8am.

Sequoia immediately warmed to his affectionate smile. His face didn't hide the truth: he fancied her. In that moment Sequoia took comfort that, despite her emotional turmoil, men still found her desirable.

'Hey Jack, how are you today?'

'All the better for seeing you Sequoia,' he said, gratefully taking hold of the paper cup. 'Best be on my way. Thanks for the coffee.'

He walked out towards the front of the café, then turned around. 'Fancy a movie tonight?'

'I'd love that Jack,' she said, watching his face light up 'but by the end of the day I'm usually dead on my feet and just want to go home and have a long bath.' The words were no sooner out of her mouth than she wished she'd said something else. She could see his imagination working overtime; could see himself in the bath beside her. Sequoia flushed, and turned towards the coffee machine, busying herself. 'Another time, perhaps?'

'Sure,' he said, his shoulders slouching, and then he scooted up the pavement.

I must learn to be gentler with men, she said to herself.

Ali joined her half an hour later, and the work day began in earnest.

Patrick made himself at home on one of the outside tables, ordering coffee by the half hour.

'You really must start giving him decaff, Sequoia. Don't want him dropping dead of a heart attack on the pavement. I used to think it was cute, him sitting there all devoted to you, but now? Nah, not cute. Pathetic.'

Sequoia raised her eyebrow. 'I don't ask him to come here and pine for me, you know!'

'Don't you?' Ali laughed. 'You're not exactly firm with him, or with Jack. Just say "no". If you don't want either of them, be clear with them. Let them move on so other women can enjoy their bodies.'

'But what if I'm wrong? What if one of them is my soul mate?' she bit her lip, nervously.

'Are you kidding me?' Ali blew out a huge breath. 'When you meet your soul mate, the feelings are reciprocated. Sequoia, when you meet the right one you don't have to ask if he's the right one. You just know!'

'There was a time I might have just agreed with that. But, not now. I doubt I'll ever know if someone's the right one for me.'

Sequoia sliced the handsome salted-caramel cheesecake into twelve equal slices, and placed them under a tear-shaped glass canopy on the front counter. She licked a little of the sauce from her fingers, brought to heaven by the sweet milky taste, and then looked over and caught Patrick looking at her admiringly, enchanted by the seductive way her mouth had taken in the caramel. Aware that she'd blushed crimson, Sequoia walked out to the back kitchen, her heart racing. There was Patrick, turned on by her few seconds of oral pleasure, and what had she been thinking about? Not caramel cheesecake, that's for certain. Her x-rated thoughts were all on Ruben.

Darn!

Pull yourself together, girl, she said to herself as she set about preparing the lunchtime specials. Sequoia assembled a sweetcorn, black bean and pumpkin casserole; baked a root-vegetable cobbler; and layered an eggplant, potato and mushroom moussaka. Each day there were three chef's specials on the chalkboard at *Treble Clef*, and this allowed her to revel in her daily dose of creativity.

Playing the piano was creative, too, and she couldn't go a day without touching the keys, but she also enjoyed the aromas and textures of food

50

preparation. This morning, though, she found herself feeling a little more than frustrated. Not a vegetable or herb passed her hands that didn't have some Ruben-memory attached to it and to her. Whether it was fine dining in London, or picnics on the beach, eating cheese and pickle sandwiches above her bakery in France, or candlelit suppers in his remote Scottish-Highland castle as they snuggled on a rug by the blazing open fire, or their days under the Tuscan sun, or his visits to her little village in France, he was there: his fingerprints all over her life, her memories, her *heart*.

For eight years she'd deconstructed memories: his touch, his smell, his taste, and now... Now what? It was like she was back to square one, only now it was going to be so much harder knowing he was in the area.

How long until their paths crossed? How long until she was looking into his eyes and trying to pretend she didn't care? That he, Ruben Hazelwood, didn't matter?

Hazelwood Hotel

Residents of the bay were in awe at the new hotel complex. It defied any criticism, and blended in beautifully to the surrounding mountains and shoreline. The architect had taken inspiration from the colours of the landscape: pink granite from the Hazards Mountains, sapphire-coloured waters of the bay, the grey-green of the eucalyptus trees, and the white sandy beaches. There was nothing about Hazelwood Hotel which conflicted with the environment. It seamlessly connected with the beautiful landscape around it, and offered a rejuvenating retreat for the rich and famous. Hazelwood was designed for those who wanted luxury in their life; for those who wanted the ultimate in pampering. For those who weren't afraid to say: *I deserve the best.*

Even before opening, it had won awards for its unique and ethical design. And what was not to love? Sequoia wondered, given that it was nestled so impeccably into the purity of the natural landscape of Coles Bay. Though she hadn't yet stepped inside, she could tell from the brochure that every inch of it came from Ruben's heart, and his passion for the Earth and nature. Despite the opulent lifestyle he grew up with, she had sensed from the beginning his great love of the outdoors. When he wasn't dining with royalty and rock stars in Michelin-star restaurants, he was mountain climbing, skiing, sailing and exploring jungles.

Photos on the brochure showed the local landscape that Sequoia had grown to love, reflected in the use of local stone and timber. Guests would be tempted to interact with the outside world, and enjoy the marine life. *Very clever*, she thought to herself. *The master of manipulation*, she said out loud.

Coles Bay, with its population of less than 200, had remained a secret to international visitors, and was one of the reasons Sequoia had chosen to settle down here, but now, with Hazelwood Hotel opening its doors, the bay would become a popular holiday spot with foreigners. They'd soon discover the mild climate, which boasted more than 300 days of sunshine a year: the main reason she'd chosen to settle here. Her life had been darkened with pain, and more than anything she wanted light.

All Sequoia had to say when Jack Breardon asked for her opinion was that it costs more to stay in that hotel for one night than she earned in take-home pay in a fortnight. He retreated at her disdain.

'But it is beautiful,' he said, trying to get her to marvel at the brochure some more.

'Yes, it's beautiful Jack. Just like a woman, people will be able to grovel at its knees, wanting more,' and she caught the vicious sarcasm coming from her mouth, and was horrified at her behaviour. Eight years of pent-up anger will do that to a girl, she told herself.

'Sorry Jack, I don't know what got into me. Just not that into the lifestyles of the rich and famous.'

'But it would be nice to stay there, wouldn't it?' he said, totally taken in by what it had to offer.

Sequoia was feeling jittery about the Ball of the Bay this weekend. Now that she knew for sure Ruben was behind the development, there'd be no escaping him. While most women would be fretting about what to wear for such an extravagant event, Sequoia wasn't bothered. Ruben had seen her naked, many times, so it wasn't as if she'd be dressing to seduce him or taunt him. No, she wouldn't be dressing for him at all, but for herself. And Jack. Dear, sweet Jack.

Each leaseholder in the bay had been offered a complimentary overnight stay in the hotel for the evening of the ball. The Ball of the Bay marked the official opening, and was to be a grand affair, unlike anything held before in the history of Coles Bay. Guests were welcome to book into their room before the ball, and settle in. Sequoia had enough experience with the Hazelwood family to know this wasn't a denim-jeans sort of place. No, this was first-class luxury for the wealthy; for those who had no idea what a litre of milk costs or what it's like to fret when rent day is around the corner and your bank account is stone dry. A place for those who own more shoes than a shoe store.

It was a world she had stepped into, and walked away from with a bitter aftertaste that she could still remember after all these years. Sequoia preferred cupcakes to caviar any day of the year.

Despite Jack's offer to go to the hotel with Sequoia, she declined and said she'd meet him there. The hotel was even more luxurious than the detailed brochure she'd inspected. Every room spoke to her of Ruben. He always had such exquisite taste: in food, clothing, décor, entertainment. She sighed, and remembered the good times and the love they shared before everything turned upside down. Before he dumped her and married another woman. A more suitable woman. *An exquisite woman.*

As Sequoia entered the foyer of Hazelwood Hotel, she was struck that such a palatial place could feel so intimate. It exuded excellence and luxury. Its client list of royalty, authors, politicians, singers and film stars meant it was already booked ahead for the next eight months. Hazelwood did not need advertising. It would rely entirely on word of mouth.

The mirrors and marble, hugged between natural stone and local timber, ensured the hotel was a masterpiece of originality. Maximum use of natural light meant there was little need for harsh fluorescents. There wouldn't be another hotel like it in the world, Sequoia thought to herself, and that made her smile. Ruben had always made a point of being one of a kind, and wasn't one to fit the mould. She reluctantly admitted defeat, and inwardly acknowledged this huge achievement. It was true: he was a person in his own right, and not just a descendant of a silver-spooned dynasty.

Escorted to her room, Sequoia was given the honeymoon suite. Ironic, she thought, but she allowed herself to revel in the luxury. It was something she hadn't experienced for a long time, and was somewhat disappointed in herself that it felt so darned good. She twirled around the room, and gave out a delighted squeal. Just for the pure fun of it, she bounced up and down on the Queen-sized bed, giggling as she collapsed. Today she wasn't twenty seven years old; she was seven.

The suite had floor-to-ceiling windows so guests could take in the expansive view of the beach and the pink-tinted granite mountains: five distinctive craggy-ragged peaks known as the Hazards.

Sequoia smiled at the beauty before her: a flock of black cockatoos feeding on the lawns of the hotel, the apricot sunset over the bay, and unspoilt Tasmanian wilderness. *Oh yes, Ruben Hazelwood has class*, she said to herself.

Bouquets of sweetly scented freesias adorned the room. They were clearly chosen by someone who knew they were Sequoia's favourite flower. *Sweet touch*, she thought, trying not to be taken in by his charm, but grateful to be bathed in such an exquisite scent. *Stop romancing me. It won't work, Ruben*, she muttered, but couldn't help smiling at the lengths he was going to.

Exotic fruits nestled in baskets around the room, and a stereo played romantic piano pieces. *He really is trying to make a statement*, she whispered to herself, and then went to place her clothes into the wardrobe. As she opened the large mirrored door, she was surprised to see a ball gown hanging there, with a note attached to the coat hanger. *Please wear this, Sequoia. For me. R x*

Her heart swooped. Just seeing that initial, and his trademark single kiss, began to undo her. *Don't do this*, she pleaded to him across the ethers. *Don't do this. I've come too far for you to unravel me.* She was about to pack up and leave when a knock came at the door.

'Who is it?' she said, flustered.

'Room service, madam.'

Sequoia indicated to the maid that she could come in, and was astonished to be given a small purple velvet box.

'Mr Hazelwood has sent this with his compliments. He'd like you to wear it tonight.'

Sequoia smiled weakly. She was supposed to be here on a date with Jack Breardon, but was being wooed by Ruben Hazelwood! And he wasn't even in the room with her. Damn him!

She was taken aback by the beautiful necklace. He'd clearly had it made just for her: orange-red imperial topaz embedded in a sterling-silver shaped treble clef. Sweet!

It was another two hours until the ball started. It was to be an intimate affair, in keeping with the nature of the hotel and of Coles Bay. There were 20 luxury rooms in the hotel, and the restaurant seated forty. The ballroom could possibly take 100 people. Many guests were coming just for the dance.

Sequoia decided to make the most of the room, and treated herself to a spa bath. She conditioned her hair with coconut milk, put on an apricot-kernel face scrub, and lay back in the warm bubbly water. Baroque music was piped through the speakers and she was lulled into a deep reverie. It had been far too long since she was this relaxed.

Bad move, she thought in hindsight. The heat of the water took her back to her Italian holiday with Ruben, at his villa in Tuscany. Surrounded by cypress trees, they were hidden from the world. They only had eyes for each other. Sequoia told Ruben how she'd been named after the giant redwood sequoia tree of California, a member of the cypress family, and how her parents had been college students and met when camping one summer at Sequoia National Park in the U.S.A. Their affair had been brief and passionate, but long enough for Sequoia to be conceived. It was a lifelong regret that she'd never met her father, and that he never knew of her existence. Her mother hadn't even known his surname before they parted ways.

In his private Italian oasis, Ruben invited Sequoia into the natural thermal pool, and under the stars they kissed. The warm water made her heady, and with giddiness she told Ruben how much she loved him. She'd seen his face change. Shock? Surprise? Gratitude? Responsibility? Relief? She couldn't figure it out. He didn't respond with words, but he beckoned her with his strong, stable and urgent body. Everything about that night: the intimacy, the beauty of the stars above, the warm and steaming natural thermal waters, and Ruben's adoration of her, marked a place in her heart. It has been one of the best times of her life.

A knock at the door startled her. Time already? Quickly slipping on the hotel's luxuriously thick towelling robe, Sequoia answered the door. Ali was there, beautiful as a Disney princess, bursting at the seams with joy.

'You're not dressed! Dinner starts in half an hour!'

'I'll be ready,' Sequoia promised, knowing she was in a war with the impatient tick, tick, tick of the clock. 'I'll see you down there.'

Where to start first? Face? She smoothed in a rich moisturising cream, followed by a thin layer of foundation and powder. She rarely wore make-up, preferring to let her natural tan emphasise her features: deep brown, almond-shaped eyes, pert nose, rosebud lips. Ruben had once told her that women paid good money to have their noses sculpted into the shape of hers. The memory made her smile. It seemed all of her memories of Ruben were having this effect on her tonight. There was another side to Ruben, and she was best to remember that! Especially tonight, for surely he'd be here at the ball.

Darkening her lashes with thick-volume mascara, and brushing a little dark brown and gold-flecked eye shadow across the lids of her eyes, she sat back and thought 'you'll do'.

Undecided about whether to wear her hair up or down, she dithered in front of the mirror. Traditionally, women wore it up when wearing ball gowns, and that is certainly how they did it across Europe at all the dances she'd been to with Ruben, but she was feeling a bit rebellious tonight. Nope, she would be leaving her hair down. Besides, she wore it up every day in the café kitchen. Sequoia took her time drying her long lustrous locks of hair, and then dabbed exotic ylang ylang essential oil onto her neck. Perfume was good, but she decided this was better. Authentic and rich. Oil seeped into a woman's skin, and set alive any man who happened to be nearby.

Carefully, she stepped into the dress. It was an unusual colour choice, she thought, but as she surveyed herself in front of the full-length mirror, she realised it was perfect for her colouring. Deep turquoise and aqua-marine shades, each merging into the other, and shimmering in the light, contrasted perfectly with her eyes and glossy hair. Strapless, with deeply plunging v-neck, cinched in at the waist, it boasted a full skirt to the floor. Sequoia reconsidered wearing the dress she'd brought with her: a simple white taffeta number. If she didn't wear the gown he'd bought for her, it would be like slapping Ruben across the face. And oh boy, did he deserve that! If she dared to be honest with herself, she had wanted to slap him for every day of pain that he'd caused. Toying with the idea for a moment, she defiantly headed back to the wardrobe to change only to be interrupted by a knock at the door.

'Jack!'

When he didn't say a word, she realised he'd never seen her wear anything other than jeans or shorts. Sure she had countless colourful blouses, and always looked terrific, but this? Sequoia almost thought she heard him groan under his breath, and could read his thoughts. A man, just like any other, she mused.

'Ready then?' she asked.

Her thoughts turned to Ruben, and she wondered how he could so accurately measure her dress size. He hadn't held her for eight years, and her body had changed enormously in that time. Five visits to the gym a week, committed to a unique cardio programme, and morning jogs on the beach, had changed her shape in many ways.

'You look exquisite. I hope you don't mind me saying so,' he asked, half apologetically. In that moment Sequoia realised Jack, as kind, gentle and lovely as he was, could never be the man for her. She liked a man who didn't apologise. A man who knew what he wanted! *A man... Shut up*, she told herself. *Just shut up!*

The dining room was a picture of elegance. Like her suite, it had floor-to-ceiling glass windows overlooking the mountains and Coles Bay. Sconces adorned the walls, candles inside them flickering; and vases filled with local flora sat upon small tables like punctuation marks in front of the pillars behind them.

The men looked dapper in their tuxedos, and the women dressed like every little girl's fantasy: Cinderella. But try as she might, Sequoia couldn't see Prince Charming anywhere. Perhaps he wasn't coming to the ball after all. Perhaps, just like the elusive media interviews, he was going to stay in the background, and have his minders inform him about the evening. The leaden weight of her heart betrayed her. Had she really wanted to see Ruben after all? So deep in thought, and confused by her disappointment, she missed most of Jack's conversation.

'Aren't you hungry?' he asked, more than once. 'You've hardly touched your food.'

'Oh', she said, looking down at the plate before her. The silver service was just as she'd remembered, and for the first time she realised that it had its place; that there were times in life when refinement could be honoured. A time for chips doused in vinegar on the beach, and a time for fine dining, silver cutlery polished until it gleamed. She thought of how she had worn glass slippers in Ruben's world, and how he had walked barefoot in her world; how different they were, and yet how alike.

Sequoia found herself enjoying being waited on. It made a refreshing change from always being the one doing the serving; she decided it was rather nice to have someone take care of your every need. Just for tonight, she'd pretend. She'd pretend that she deserved such a lifestyle.

For starters, Sequoia had chosen roasted artichoke with chipotle aioli, and for the first time she realised how often she'd integrated some of the meals she'd shared with Ruben into the more casual food she cooked up at *Treble Clef*. Reluctantly she pulled herself out of her prince and princess daydreams.

For her main meal: butternut squash and pear ravioli with rosemary sauce; its succulence inevitably brought her back to her days in the Tuscan sunshine falling so deeply in love with her lover. And then her fateful descent into the Underworld, her nightmare with the dark days, was reignited with her conscious choice of pomegranate sorbet: the fruit of the Greek goddess, Persephone.

As she ate, Sequoia tucked ideas from the presentation, and the delicate garnishes, into the back of her mind where she mentally rearranged them for the casual diners who would wander into *Treble Clef* looking for good food. Sequoia acknowledged that she was a magpie food collector: little ideas and touches here and there, and then she branded her identity onto them. The Sequoia Touch, she liked to call it.

The string quartet, which had played love songs throughout dinner, gave way to a small orchestra in the ballroom.

Jack took Sequoia's hand, and as he escorted her towards the dance floor she could see he was beside himself with pride. But all Sequoia could think of was: was she cheating on Patrick, by coming to the ball with Jack? After all, as he said, he'd been waiting for six months. One thing was clear: tomorrow she'd tell Patrick that there was no future between them. It was time for him to move on. And for her to move forward, too. She owed him that much, though she wasn't looking forward to breaking his heart.

And then her thoughts turned to her kitten, Adagio, and if she was being well looked after by her next-door neighbour. This was their first night apart. Sequoia laughed inside at her emerging motherly instincts, and was completely unaware that Jack had already led her onto the dance floor and they were spinning to a waltz.

Dimly lit for maximum ambience, the ballroom was alive with dancers in their finery. Wooden floorboards were sprung to suit the best professional dancers who would perform here for the hotel guests. The chandeliers hung low, and the orchestra played. For the first two dances, she smiled brightly, but then a Strauss waltz—one of her mother's favourites—caught her in mid-belly, and she choked back a tear. But before Jack, who looked like the cat who got the cream, noticed, someone else had. A tap on Jack's shoulder had him sidelined by Ruben Hazelwood.

Jack walked sullenly to the cocktail bar, as his dance partner became someone else's.

'Who are the tears for, my darling?' Ruben whispered into her ear.

Unable to answer, Sequoia was aware that this was still the Ruben she'd loved with all her heart, but he was different, too. Older. Stronger. *Jaded*, somehow. Oh man, he sure smelt good! Lost, lost entirely in the scent of his spice aftershave, and its deep undertones of the the great outdoors, she was reminded of the Bavarian forest where they'd made love. Ruben held her close, and she could feel herself falling.

'My mother,' she whispered. 'Strauss was her favourite. Why are you here?' she asked, staring right into his eyes.

'This is my hotel,' he said matter of factly, lifting his hand to wipe her tear.

'No, why are you *here*? In Tasmania. Did you follow me?'

'You must have known I'd follow you to the ends of the earth, my darling. Always.'

Feeling fury rise in her being, she tried to pull away, but his hold was too tight.

'I'm not your darling,' she hissed, 'I wonder if I ever was?' And her words cut through him like a million glass splinters. When his face registered pain, she felt an ounce of pleasure.

'I will do everything I can to win you back. Everything.'

'You can't buy me, Ruben.'

'I knew that from the first day we met,' and he pulled her forward and kissed her softly on the forehead. 'Still as feisty as ever,' he smiled. 'My feisty fairy you've been kissing too many men for my liking,' he snarled gently. 'We'll have to put an end to that.'

For a second, she was about to protest, and then thought better of it. Why not let him believe she was seeing other people? See how he liked it.

Scouring the perimeter of the ballroom, she couldn't see Jack anywhere. Not that she was sure she wanted him to rescue her.

'He's gone,' Ruben said softly. 'So you can stop fighting me now. It's just us.'

Conversation with Ruben was minimal, but he didn't let her go for the rest of the night, and even in between dances, he held her in his tight embrace.

Ali swung by them several times. Sequoia could tell that her best friend was studying Ruben right down to his shiny handmade Italian shoes.

'You always looked beautiful to me, Sequoia. I know the British Press crucified you with their descriptions. It was mean, cruel, nasty, *unnecessary*, and completely false. *Everything* about your body was perfect to me. The way you looked, the way you smelled, how you felt under my hands...' he groaned. 'Every last curve, the voluptuous roundness of your breasts and hips, and the line of...'

'Ruben, *stop!*'

His thumb caught the tears in her eyes.

'I don't want to be reminded of that time in my life.'

'I want to remind you of what we had,' he insisted. 'Of what was special between us.'

'Then don't bring up the tabloids! That's the quickest way to see me walk out the door!'

'Let me remind you of something else then,' he smiled, hoping to calm her down. With breath, warm against her skin, he whispered memories of making love to her in the highlands of Scotland, in his castle.

The king-sized bed, the open fire, the views of the mountains, the deer bounding across the expansive, park-like, gardens; the feel of her skin, the sounds of pleasure she made. When Sequoia went weak at the knees, she knew he felt it, and that she was under his spell. Barely audible, but just loud enough that she could hear him describing every last inch of her body; the valleys, mountains, rivers and mounds. She had to get out of here before he completely destroyed any control she'd hoped to exercise.

'I want to remind you of everything you gave up when you ran away,' he whispered into her ear.

'Stop it,' she hissed. 'Stop it. I'm not yours, and I never was. I never will be! Now let me go!' she ordered under her breath. Was he even listening to her? she wondered, as he pulled her even closer to his tense and rigid body.

'Me thinketh that the woman protesteth too much.' And he smiled in a way that made her even angrier. Why did he have to be so darned gorgeous? So captivating?

Why did she want nothing more than for him to remove her clothing and leave her begging for consumation? This wasn't the woman she'd become!

'Now,' he said, rather too smugly for her liking. 'That puppy dog who keeps hanging around you? It's time for him to go.'

'Puppy dog? How did you know we called him puppy dog?' she said, more concerned with Patrick's description than what Ruben was asking; was ordering.

'What else could he be with that mop of curly, shaggy hair and his lovesick eyes? Get rid of him Sequoia.'

'No,' she said firmly. 'I will not.' She wasn't going

to give Ruben the satisfaction of knowing that it had been her intention to send him on his way tomorrow anyway. No, she was going to make Ruben pay for what he put her through!

'And the old grandpa? He's more than love-sick. He's besotted. I don't want you to see him any more. Not tonight, and not tomorrow' he said firmly. If he thought there'd be no argument, he underestimated who he was talking to. Sequoia might be shy, but she sure as hell was feisty when she set her mind to it.

'I hate your arrogance. You're so smug. You think you can just click your fingers and have what you want. But you can't have me, and you can't tell me who I can and can't see. Jack's a good man; and unlike you, he cares enough about me that he would never hurt me!'

She could see him reel, as if she'd slapped him across the face. Sequoia couldn't help but feel a hint of satisfaction. Finally, she was finding her feet again, feeling empowered. Ruben was not going to railroad her into bed.

'You can hate me all you like, but we both know that deep down you want me. You know what you've been missing, and you know I'm the only man who can make you feel this way.' The gravelly tones of his voice rumbled down into the furthest reaches of her body.

'I came here with one man: Jack. I'm hardly going to go home with another man. You don't know me very well at all if you think I'd do that!' She spat the words out, still trying to writhe free from his firm hands.

'I'm not asking you to go home with me, Sequoia! I'm asking you to come to my bed.'

'No!' And she stamped her foot, just loud enough for him to hear.

Ruben let her go, and as he walked away, his stride

was brisk and purposeful, Sequoia stood shaking, and alone, on the ballroom floor. The orchestra was packing up, and the guests had left. It was several minutes before she regained any semblance of composure. How did he exert such a powerful effect on her? She was putty in his hands.

Sequoia orientated herself, and walked back to her suite. The sooner she left this hotel, the better! She'd grab her overnight bag, and would be straight out the front door; but first, she had to find Jack and apologise. The poor man! He didn't deserve to be discarded like that.

At first, she knocked gingerly on his bedroom door, but there was no answer. She tried several times, but didn't want to disturb the other patrons, so tiptoed up to her room. As she entered, she saw an envelope on the floor with her name handwritten on the front.

Dear Sequoia,
You looked absolutely stunning tonight. It was a joy to dine with you, and I would have liked to spend the whole evening dancing together. I had no idea that you knew Ruben Hazelwood, and I'm disappointed that you've never shared this information with me. I've decided not to stay tonight. I couldn't bear to watch you both dining at breakfast! Jack.

Ouch! Was it that obvious that she and Ruben shared a past? A physical past? Suppressing the urge to scream, she channelled her anger into collecting her possessions and packing them into her overnight bag. Jack could wait till the morning for her apology. But first, she needed to go home and get some sleep. That's when she heard the door opening. It could only be one person. Like the galloping hooves of a wild stallion, her heart pounded deep within her chest. How would she ever leave if he came into the room?

'Please don't leave,' he said softly, when he saw her packing. 'I won't take you against your will, you know that, Sequoia, but stop fighting me on this. We both want to be together'

'Ruben, if a woman says no she means no. And no matter what you may or may not have done to hurt me in the past, I do know you'd never do that to me, but please understand that there...'

A torrid rush of bodily impulses overruled her mind. Thoughts vanished, and she found herself magnetised by the scorching promise he held firm and hard against her. Her blood was boiling, no longer from anger but desire. *He could have her without even trying.* Who was she to resist? Eight years may have passed, but she was still the same woman underneath. The same girl, now a woman, who was like butter in the sunshine when he touched her. And he was touching her now. Not in the gentle way she remembered; no, this was different. He was impatient. Back then, back in France, when he gifted her with the first sexual experience of her life, it had been so tender, affectionate and kind-hearted. Now she could feel his animalistic desires, and they had no intention of being dimmed. Slowly the zip of her ball gown was inched down, falling to the floor like a crumpled fairy. Ruben wanted to slow down, he wanted to savour the view: one he hadn't seen in a very long time; to be slow, gentle, kind, but he didn't want to wait.

'Wise move not wearing a bra,' he growled as his mouth reached down to her other breast.

She may have said no, but how could she mean no when her nipples hardened in his mouth? How could she mean no when her body was pressing into his? Her moans were a plea. They were saying that she wanted him in every way possible.

'Ruben,' she moaned gently as he picked her up and carried her to the bed.

'Say you want me. Say that you want me in your bed,' he said.

'I...' and she yelped with the pleasure coursing through her veins.

'Tell me yes,' Ruben said, trying to stifle his urge to take her there and then. She'd been right about one thing: he would never force a woman.

'Sequoia, do you want me to make love to you?'

As tears fell down her face and across her shoulders, Ruben let her go. She turned away from him, face down, on the bed.

'Why are you crying?' he asked, his voice a mix of frustration and empathy.

She couldn't answer. Surely he must understand? Sequoia realised that she'd waited eight years for them to be reunited, but she never, *ever*, thought it would be like this.

Carefully sitting down on the bed beside her, Ruben pulled her close. Gently, softly, and kindly. He cursed under his ragged breath.

'I'm sorry,' he said. 'That was wrong. It's clear that you have no interest in me whatsoever, and your reaction was purely physical. I was an idiot to think that you'd still care for me all these years later.'

Ruben couldn't let her go though. He was shocked by his possessiveness. If she didn't want him, that was one thing, but he wasn't going to let her run off to Jack! Or the poodle! Sequoia was worth more than both of those feeble men put together.

With soft fingers, he traced the outline of her face.

'Will you ever forgive me?' he asked, his voice near breaking point, as he searched her eyes. Ruben leant in and kissed her; his lips gentle, inviting, luring her towards him. 'You deserve better than me. You always have.' Then, he kissed her once, slowly, on the forehead, and left the room.

The night was long, and she kicked herself for not going home. There was no point staying in the hotel, but for some reason she wanted to stay in the room. It smelt of Ruben: his spicy and earthy aftershave, his sexuality, his heat. Sequoia didn't want to let go of him. Maybe he'd come back?

Why did she fight him? Why did she have to make him pay? Now she'd never get the chance to feel his arms around her again. She slid onto the silky sheets, her bare skin tingling, and memories came flooding back.That night, her body tumbled and tossed and twisted; blankets were thrown, and Sequoia spent the silent hours of darkness imagining him in her bed. In her mind, she created a fictional evening of love, lust and non-resistance, and slowly let her thoughts turn to their holiday in Tuscany all those years ago: Pleasure and pain. Bliss and bereavement.

Under The Tuscan Sun

Ruben had convinced Sequoia to take some time out from the bakery, and he'd employed a replacement baker. They would holiday at his castle in Scotland; near the Bavarian Black Forest in Germany; and spend some time in London, taking in operas, ballet and restaurants, and then finish with a vacation at his Tuscan Villa. Sequoia was reluctant to leave the little boulangerie in someone else's hands, but she knew Ruben was right: she needed a change of scenery, and some time out after her mother's death.

The Italian villa nestled in a beautiful countryside location, perfect for his celebrity friends who wanted to holiday away from the prying lenses of the media. Ruben didn't come here very often, but when he did it was for the express purpose of peace and quiet.

Each day they enjoyed taking long walks through vineyards, up long roads garlanded by poplar trees, and ate picnics in the sunshine. They were inseparable, and though neither of them had said it yet, they were in love with each other. There was no question.

By day, they'd hold hands and talk for hours, sharing their past, their dreams, and kissing. They were always kissing: long, slow, tender and deeply desirous. There wasn't anything, she came to realise, that he wouldn't do for her. It warmed her heart when Ruben showed her places where he played as a child, and in her heart she imagined their children playing there one day. They were waited on by staff who tended to their every whim. Initially, Sequoia was uncomfortable, but she was beginning to accept that this was his way of life, and she stopped resisting.

Under the stars, they'd relax in the natural thermal pool. The heat of the water, though, was no match for the heat which sizzled between their bodies. The twinkle of the stars above was no competition for the light in their eyes.

On their last night together, Ruben carried Sequoia, naked warm and wet from the thermal pool, into the bedroom they shared. It was palatial, with an oak four-poster bed, overlooking the mountains. Large, wood-framed, glass doors opened onto a wide balcony with terracotta tiles. A wrought-iron table and chairs, and fabric porch swing, lent to the relaxed atmosphere. The fresh evening breeze invited itself into their privacy, and the cool wind teased Sequoia's bare breasts, urging them to harden. But Ruben had already got there first. Seductively cupping a voluptuous breast with one hand, his other reached around her waist, drawing them closer together.

'I need you,' he murmured into her hair. And groaning, he said it again. '*I need you.*'

Her body, eager to please, even more eager to be pleased, beckoned him.

Sequoia could hear the distant drums. The musician in her heard them every time they made love… at first, they were at a distance, and then *pa dum, pa dum, pa dum*…the gentle rhythm getting louder, harder, pounding, until it became so loud it was deafening. Her body pulsed, convulsed; she arched her back, she trembled. If there was anything in this life that Ruben excelled at, it was arousing Sequoia. That first night in Paris, and every time their bodies came together, created a bond that neither of them ever wanted to break.

Sequoia likened her body to an instrument, no less than a piano or violin. Ruben's touch was like music to her, and as he strummed, his fingers brought her to ecstasy. Crescendo! Drugged by his touch, she fought hard to keep her eyes open. After lovemaking, they lay in each other's arms, whispering over the pillows, before falling asleep like kittens in a ball.

They hadn't long been asleep when Ruben's mobile phone woke them from their post-lovemaking bliss.

'I see,' he said harshly to the person at the end of the phone. 'I see. Of course.'

Sequoia rubbed her eyes, and sat up in bed, trying to read the time: 3.23am.

When he hung up the phone, she could see he was visibly shaken.

'Ruben? What's the matter?'

'Go back to sleep.' His voice was gruff.

Taken aback by his harshness, she found herself shaking. How dare he be rude after what they had just shared? How could he cut her off like that when she'd just been so physically and emotionally open with him?

When she made eye contact, a silver tear glistened on her cheek.

'Oh honey, I'm so sorry,' he said, and wrapped his arms around Sequoia as if he was never going to let her go. Only, he *did* let her go. And he was going to live the rest of his life with regret.

'I don't have time to explain now.' He cursed, and hit the bed with a furious fist.

Sequoia jumped, startled.

'I have to go back to England. Urgently. I'll call François to meet you at the airport.' Ruben pulled out his wallet. 'Here's your plane ticket back to Paris. And...' She could see him stifling tears. What on earth was wrong?

73

'And there's plenty of money for you in case you need it. Get a taxi from here to the airport. Roberta's number is on the fridge. She'll come ánd get the keys from you when you're ready to leave. François will meet you in Paris, and drive you back to the bakery. I'll be in touch as soon as I can. I promise. You have my word on that.'

Within half an hour, Ruben was gone.

Sequoia sat up in bed, stunned. No explanation, nothing. She looked around the room. This place was meaningless without Ruben here to share it with her. And Sequoia let herself cry. She cried softly, at first, and then she howled. Where had he gone? Why didn't he take her with him? It wasn't like he couldn't fly her back to England with him. Didn't he trust her with whatever the urgent problem was?

The following morning, after a restless sleep, she awoke to the smell of frying eggs and tomatoes. Roberta must have let herself in. Sequoia delayed going into the large open-planned farmhouse kitchen, and instead, pottered around the bedroom packing up her suitcase. She'd been away from France for two months, enjoying her whirlwind romance and travels around Europe. England had been torture; the way the press had treated her when she attended several charity events with Ruben was brutal. Sequoia wasn't sure she'd ever recover from their vicious headlines.

For a while she deliberated over whether to pack up Ruben's clothes. In his haste, he'd only taken an overnight bag.

Sequoia began folding up his shirts, trousers, and underwear. Then she opened the top drawer and took out his socks and silk briefs. Her hand felt something hard, and she pushed away some items of underwear; and there, at the back, lay a small, navy-blue velvet box. Carefully prising it open, she was stunned to see an exquisite diamond ring. It was simple, but beautiful. Next to it was a card depicting two lovers, side by side and holding hands near a river. Ruben's handwriting read:

My beautiful Sequoia,
you are the only thing in my life
that has ever made sense.
I love you. R x

Tears of joy slipped from her eyes, looking for someone, anyone, to catch them. Everything would be okay, now. They were getting married! And as she let out a laugh, Sequoia allowed the deliriously happy feeling to permeate her whole being.

Roberta knocked on the door. 'Madame, would you like breakfast in your room or on the balcony?'

'On the balcony,' Sequoia called out. With hope in her heart, now, she wanted to savour the Italian views she'd enjoyed so much with Ruben. Yes, she wanted to remember this time in Italy for the rest of her life. She'd never been so happy. *Ruben loved her.*

In a daydream, she travelled back to France. Nothing could possibly burst the bubble of love she was dancing in. François greeted her in the limousine, and they chatted happily all the way back to the bakery.

'He made you a happy woman, didn't he?' François smiled. 'You are glowing.'

'Oh I'm very happy. I just want to tell the whole world how in love I am.' And she gave him a little peck on the cheek.

He unpacked her bags and carried them to the front door.

'Shall I take them in for you?' François asked.

'No, I can manage. Thank you François,' she said affectionately, and pecked him once again on his freshly shaven cheek.

The following morning, she got up early to help the baker, and to catch up on village news. The next few days went by in a dream, but by the end of the week Sequoia found herself getting twitchy, a bit irritated. Why hadn't Ruben phoned? After all, he promised he'd be in touch. He gave his *word*.

A month later, and there was still no word from Ruben. The happiness she'd felt upon leaving Tuscany had all but evaporated.

Sundays were her only days off at the boulangerie, so she was surprised when a knock came sharply at the front door at 8am. Drowsily, she walked downstairs from her home, and into the shop, then unlocked the door. It was the village priest, looking ashen.

'Are you okay Sequoia?' he asked kindly.

'Okay? Why do you ask?' she struggled to understand his concern.

Slowly, he held up a British tabloid paper. The words before her made Sequoia fall to the ground. Seconds later, she came to as the young priest shook her face and called her name.

'Sequoia! Sequoia! Sequoia!'

Slowly, she sat up, and orientated herself back into the surroundings. Reaching over for the paper, she read each word slowly, just to make sure she wasn't having a nightmare:

Hazelwood Heir Marries Stunning Mystery Woman
And the subtitle read: *Dumps fat bakery girl.*

Recoiling, she whispered 'It can't be true. He was going to marry *me!*'

'I don't understand what this is about,' the priest said, holding her hand. 'I'm a good judge of character, and this isn't like Ruben. I know I don't know him well, but what I do know is that he loves you. I don't understand this. I'm confused.' He placed a handkerchief into her trembling hands.

'I'm sorry,' she said over and over again as she tried to stifle her sobs. 'He's never actually said that he loves me. Well, not to my face. I just assumed he did by his actions, and by a card he'd written.' She looked up at the priest sensing the hopelessness he felt. 'I could see it in his eyes,' and she blushed, 'and in his *touch.*'

The priest stood up and said, 'You need to get to the bottom of this. And Sequoia, you're not fat!'

The next morning a courier arrived at 7.30 with a special delivery which required her signature. No sooner had she signed for it, than she saw the envelope was from Ruben. The sight of his neat writing caused her heart to pounce. Three words on the envelope: *Sequoia Lissen. URGENT.* She waved the courier off, and then screwed the envelope up in her hand using every last ounce of anger. *Go to hell*, she spat, and without giving it another thought, threw the envelope into the wood-fired oven. Ashes. She wasn't interested in what he had to say. He was out of her life now, and she never wanted to see him again.

Sequoia had never felt more alone in her life. Her mother was dead, her lover was gone. *Her lover was gone!* Now in the arms of another woman, and making love to her. Ruben was doing all the things to her that he had done with Sequoia. She cringed at the image in her head, and let out a wounded yelp, like a dog that had been kicked.

It took just four weeks to sell the bakery, and for the paperwork to be finalised. As she stood at her mother's gravestone, tears trickling down her cheeks, Sequoia cried 'I never thought I'd leave you, Mama. I'm so sorry. Sleep well.' And she carefully placed down a bunch of tulips and walked away.

Four weeks, just four weeks to let go of her mother's family ancestry. All loose ends tidied up. The phone hadn't stopped ringing since the news about Ruben's marriage had made the papers. Sequoia called in friends from the village to field the calls. They weren't bakery orders being phoned in, but hungry tabloid journalists wanting the scoop on the millionaire love rat who dumped her in Tuscany. There were TV offers, and calls from newspapers around the world.

Sequoia chopped her long brown hair right off to chin length, razor-cut style, and bleached it blonde. On her European passport, she stayed in Germany for a few weeks, then to the U.S.A. Then, she travelled to Australia on her Australian passport, and silently gave thanks to her mother for always insisting she take advantage of her maternal grandmother's origins. Sequoia deconstructed everything, including her memories, and disappeared without a trace. Over the space of a couple of months she lost two stone in weight. Her round, soft feminine curves became harder and edgy, and as the weight whittled off, her body became almost boy-like. She didn't care. Transformation was important to her. There was no going back.

Play For Me

Sequoia studied the ink on the parchment paper, blinked, and wondered if it was real. Was he trying to be cruel? Surely he must know what such a note would do to her? How it would remind her of the first night he ever made love to her? Why now? Why did he want her to play for him? It was utterly ridiculous!

Dear Sequoia,
Please come and play for me.
Love, R x

It wasn't the first time in her life that she'd thrown out a letter from Ruben, but she hoped it would be the last time. Sitting on the sofa, trying to read a magazine, she felt restless. A little TV watching didn't settle her either. Sequoia brewed herself a cup of chamomile tea; but still, she was restless. Just as she was about to go to bed she decided, instead, to sit at the upright piano and play. 'I won't play for you Ruben, I'll play for myself!' And for the next few hours, she played.

Sequoia's mother had always hoped her daughter would give up the bakery and become a concert pianist, but she didn't want to leave her mother or her life in rural France to live a life on the road. Besides, she enjoyed her creature comforts, and home cooking, and the familiar day-to-day rhythm of their simple and peaceful life. Not that it was an easy one, waking up early six days a week. But, oh how she loved who she became when she played Strauss waltzes and Mozart sonatas. Her whole body swayed and thrilled with each feel of emotion the tune ignited in her. Caught, lost, consumed by the melodies and harmonies, she found herself relaxing.

As she began a Schubert serenade, Ruben's face came into her mind. Even though she'd come to the piano to put thoughts of him to rest, somehow he was here again, in her mind: How he'd made love to her so tenderly when she was crying one night, still deeply grieving her mother's passing. She wondered how the man who had been so concerned with her emotional wellbeing could end up being so heartless, so cruel. Sniffing away the tears, she tried to remove the memory of his hands on her body. It was, of course, easier said than done.

Sequoia had no idea that for the past hour Ruben had been sitting on the porch swing on her front verandah. Listening. Smiling. And, at times, crying, as he listened to her play.

When Ruben realised that she wouldn't come to him to play, he decided he'd come to her instead. Ruben didn't dare knock on her door. Rejection was not something he needed right now. Many of the pieces she played were ones they'd danced to during the charity balls they'd attended together. Did she play them on purpose or by coincidence? he wondered. Either way, he didn't mind. They were together, in his mind, dancing, swaying, kissing...and at the end of every dance they went back home and made love. They were good days, he recollected. Heady days of passionate lovemaking, and excitement at sharing new experiences together. Never, did he imagine, that they'd ever be apart. How had it all gone so horribly wrong? he wondered, as he listened to a concerto come to life beneath her fingers. He'd give anything to walk right in there and scoop her up in his arms. But he knew it was pointless. She'd fight him off. And then she did something which took him completely by surprise. He'd only ever known her to play classical and baroque pieces, but suddenly she switched to jazz, and he could hear her singing. Her voice was deep and sultry, and the words *Someone to Watch Over Me* tugged at his heart.

Ruben wanted to break down the door. He wanted to be the one to watch over her. He wanted to *be* over her, too. But he had to be honest with himself: Sequoia had moved on. It wasn't him she was singing about. It occurred to him that he'd never heard her sing before, and he found her voice doing all sorts of things to his body. It was time to go home. Time for a cold shower. Damn it!

Hungry

The end of the work day saw Sequoia was wiping down the front counter of the Treble Clef café, and putting things in order for the following morning. Ali had left five minutes earlier. Sequoia was humming to an old Billy Vera and the Beaters tune: *Have I Told you Lately that I Love You?* With her back to the front door, and her voice getting louder, she didn't hear anyone walk into the café.

It was only when the gravelly voice she knew so well said 'Hello Sequoia', did she jump around, startled.

'We're closed,' she said, fumbling with the hem of her blouse. 'We closed ten minutes ago.'

'I'm hungry, Sequoia.'

But she knew, just knew, that it wasn't food he was after. Like prey before a predator, even though she was in her own territory, she was afraid to run. Where would she run to anyway?

Those familiar dark-green eyes penetrated hers. 'I'm hungry.'

'There are other eateries on the bay. And surely your hotel must have something you can eat?'

'I don't live there, Sequoia. I want some real food. I want *your* food.'

'We're closed,' she said, but he was already on her side of the counter, reaching for her. When their lips found each other, her eyes fluttered, and then closed; and within a microsecond, she could feel herself disappearing into the world of Ruben Hazelwood. If there was such a thing as heaven, she was there.

Quickly regaining her senses, she pushed him away, even though her instincts told her to take him while she could.

'I don't kiss married men!' she snapped.

'Didn't seem to stop you after the ball. If memory serves me correctly, you rather enjoyed kissing me then.'

'Ruben...'

'Stop resisting me. Let me eat, and then I'll leave.'

Sequoia knew she was fighting a losing battle. *Just feed the man and he'll leave*, said the voice inside her head.

'What do you want from me? I was happy here! I *am* happy here. Why did you have to come along and ruin everything?' she snapped, trying to let anger override her sadness and despair.

'Have I ruined everything Sequoia?' he asked, lifting her chin to look into her watery eyes. 'What, exactly, have I ruined?'

'My peace and equilibrium!'

When he let her go, she headed into the kitchen. Ruben was just a step behind her.

'What's on the menu?' he asked, changing the subject. 'I haven't eaten all day.'

Within a minute, she rustled up some tomato and balsamic salad with grilled zucchini, halloumi and black olives.

'That's the best I can do at this hour of the day,' she said, half apologetically.

'Looks perfect. Sit down with me while I eat.'

Why did it sound like an order and not a request?

'I've got tidying up to do,' she argued.

'Sit, Sequoia. Sit with me.'

Imitating a tempestous toddler, she scraped her shoes begrudgingly across the floor, and then sat opposite him at a table for two.

'Get rid of the angry pout, Sequoia. You're far

prettier when you smile,' he said, a smirk on the corner of his lips; and his hand reached out for hers just as she was about to leave the table.

'Stop fighting me. Just sit with me while I eat. I want to talk to you.'

'I have nothing to say to you Ruben. I stopped having anything to say to you eight years ago when you left me for another woman. No, you didn't leave me for her. You married her! *Nothing* to say at all.'

There was satisfaction in watching him flinch but how could he argue with the truth? He'd left Sequoia in his villa in Italy, and married another woman in London. There was no denying that he had been, as the press reported, a love *rat*. As he sat before Sequoia, the first true love of his life, Ruben felt ashamed. He knew there was nothing he could ever do to make up for the pain his actions had caused.

'I have something to say to you, however, and I would appreciate if you'd do me the courtesy of letting me talk.' His voice was firm, and she found herself feeling like a reprimanded school girl.

She sighed, and resignedly agreed to listen.

'I have bought the entire stretch of shops around the bay.'

'Buying the world again, Ruben?' she asked sarcastically. 'Is there anything you can't buy?'

'Yes, it seems there is.'

She flinched, and pulled her hand away.

'I'm your new landlord.'

Did he have to look so pleased with the prospect?

'So? What are you going to do? Put up the price of the lease? Boot me out? What?'

'No price hike. No booting out. The only change will be that the lease will be extended to five years, rather than being signed annually.'

'Five *years*?' She was speechless. '*Five* years? Is it necessary to have that hold over us?' And as the words tumbled out of her mouth she suddenly realised what he was up to.

'I thought you'd appreciate having that sort of security?' he said charmingly, and she resisted being taken in by his smile.

'It's too long. If the economy falls flat, if there's a change in my personal circumstances...'

'You mean if you marry some guy and don't want to be tied to the café anymore?'

'Yes. No...I mean, it's just too long.'

'Take it or leave it Sequoia. The choice is yours.' He continued eating his meal. 'This salad is brilliant. Perhaps we could tempt you to work at Hazelwood, overseeing the kitchen?'

'Are you kidding? I have no interest in feeding a bunch of rich, arrogant...' And she shut up as soon as she saw his face falling. He'd complimented her, and she'd taken it as an insult. Sequoia wanted to hurt him, but not this way. Not when he was actually being kind.

'I'm sorry,' she said sincerely. 'For some reason you're bringing out the worst in me.'

'And yet I used to bring out the best in you.'

'Yeah, well things changed didn't they?'

'Sequoia...' but he didn't continue. Instead, she felt him search her eyes looking for clues, looking for a sign that would give him hope. Something. Anything. A shred. A memory.

'Stop looking at me Ruben. It unnerves me.'

'Why is that Sequoia?'

'I feel like you can see right through me.'

'And can I?'

'I don't know. You tell me!'

'Well the food was lovely,' he said, a little while later. 'Now I'd like you to play for me.' And he sat back in his chair, loosening his dark purple tie, changing the subject without another thought. 'Feed me with your music. Play for me like you used to. I've missed that.'

'Ruben, I'm not your slave!'

'Play for me,' and he said it so softly, so sincerely, that she found herself sitting upon the velvet-covered piano stool offering him Beethoven's *Moonlight Sonata*. It was a joy playing for Ruben again not that she was going to tell him that. From time to time she looked over, and the admiration and appreciation in his eyes had her melting. All over again.

Sequoia saw him glance at his watch. 'That was beautiful. Thank you Sequoia.' When he walked over to kiss her, she stepped back and he didn't come any closer.

'The amended lease will be ready for you to sign tomorrow. I'll drop it off at the end of the working day,' and he left the café without another word.

Sequoia was dumbfounded. She'd played for him for more than two hours, and now he was gone. Just like that?

What the hell was going on? Push and pull. Cat and mouse. She wanted him, oh yes she wanted him. If only he knew that he could have taken her right there on top of the baby-grand piano. So why did she recoil? Why did she give him the wrong message? Curses were tossed into the salty evening air as she walked home that night.

Dinner By Candlelight

Sequoia was on edge all day. Ruben Fever was spreading through the kitchen of *Treble Clef,* hotter than the gas flame on the stove, and disrupting everything like an 8.5 earthquake. Today, of all days, she couldn't wait for Ali to leave. At four, Ali was out the door like a strike of lightning. Sequoia was secretly relieved. She needed to be on her own and to be with her thoughts without someone intruding every two minutes. Ruben would be coming by with the paperwork, and she wanted to mentally prepare herself for seeing him again, and for having a clear head as she read the small print. Without even realising what she was doing, she cooked a meal for him, just in case. Just in case he was hungry.

Sequoia gathered together some eggplants, cinnamon, ginger and mushrooms, and created an eggplant Bolognese. She had some red wine in the pantry, and brought it out to the table she'd set for him.

Did she really have to light a candle though? Yes, she said. A storm was brewing, and the pewter clouds gathering on the bay made her shiver. The candle would bring cosiness to the café. Not that she was sure she wanted to please her new landlord!

Ruben didn't arrive till 7pm. Sequoia was furious. End of the work day, he'd said. If she'd known that she'd be in the café for three hours after it closed just waiting for him, she'd have refused.

Finally, he sauntered in, looking tired but devilishly handsome.

Eight years had only added to his appeal. How was she going to keep a straight head? A business head?

'This looks lovely,' Ruben said, admiring the table she'd set for him. 'I hope you're going to join me?'

'Would you like me to?' she asked, hesitantly.

'Of course. We *can* mix business with pleasure, you know,' and his warm smile caught her off guard.

Sequoia was all set to be firm, strong and to stand her ground, but already she was feeling like a naughty schoolgirl. Oh how she hated that feeling!

With oven mitts to protect her hands, she carried out a small casserole dish and placed it on the table. One more trip to the kitchen, and she returned with a pottery container of steaming basmati rice, and then opened the red wine.

They didn't speak for a few minutes, and then Sequoia asked 'Did you bring the paperwork then?'

'Yes,' was all he said.

Once again she could feel herself flushing in his presence. She studied him while he sipped the wine, and could feel him mentally undressing her until she was utterly naked.

The silence continued for another few minutes, and it was driving Sequoia crazy. 'Why aren't you talking?' she finally asked, exasperated.

'When I'm with you, Sequoia, I don't need to talk. I just want to enjoy having you near me.'

Even in the dim candlelight, she reckoned he could see her cheeks flush. Why am I embarrassed? We've had many times of just enjoying each other in silence.

'Well you're not here to enjoy my company Ruben. You're here to show me the contract I have to sign.'

'Right then, let's get down to business if that's what you really want,' he said, and then reached into his black brief case.

'I want a hands-on role as the landlord,' he said, passing her the lease to sign.

'But we never saw Kevin Cooper. He trusted me to just get on with my business. What do you mean, *hands on?*' Palpitations beneath her ribs threatened to derail her. She wondered if he meant it literally. And with those thoughts she remembered his hands, and what they did to her, what they were capable of doing to her. The slight sigh under her breath was a blatant giveaway that she was just as susceptible as ever.

'Take your time reading through the document.'

Sequoia read through, line by line, trying to decipher the legalese.

'Perhaps my solicitor should be looking through this for me,' she muttered, and then saw what he meant by hands-on landlord. Surely he wasn't asking her to sign an agreement that allowed him to meet with her on the *Treble Clef* premises each Friday evening to discuss the business, and how it was performing in the heart of Coles Bay? The business arrangement would include a shared meal, and Sequoia playing the piano for him.

'This is ludicrous. This isn't a business contract Ruben. I can't believe your legal team would even draw up something so stupid!' Flustered, her skin reddening all over again, she stood up. 'You can't take me hostage Ruben.' Her hands were on her hips, defiant and strong.

'As I said Sequoia, take it or leave it.' Ruben was so calm, so sure of himself, that she wanted to scream.

'Are you having weekly progress reports with the other leaseholders? Do they have to play for you?'

'No, I've just increased their rent by twenty percent instead.' He looked so darned smug!

'Ruben, why are you doing this? You had your chance to be with me. You traded me unceremoniously for a more experienced woman. Do you think I'm more experienced now? Is that it? What?'

It took all her reserves not to throw a plate into the window. 'What do you *want* from me?'

Ruben stood up, and closed the space between them. 'I know you're angry, and you have every right to be.' Within seconds she was in his arms, her fury being kissed away and transmuted into red-blooded desire.

'Ruben...' All her energy was in another part of her body.

'Will you sign it?' he asked, breaking free for a moment.

Sequoia felt dizzy. She wasn't thinking straight.

'Five years of weekly dinners with you? Will you be kissing me like this every Friday night, too?'

'If you want me to,' he said, and let her go.

As she fought to steady her jelly-like legs, she said 'You don't own me Ruben. Just remember that!'

'I've always known that Sequoia. I've always known that.'

The lease was pushed across the table, and Sequoia took the fountain pen he offered.

'Am I signing my life away?' she asked, looking into his eyes again.

'I'm not holding a gun to your head,' his smiled.

Trembling, and unable to steady her hand, she blew out a long breath.

'Sit down Sequoia. I've got all the time in the world to wait till you're back in control of your senses.' Ruben let out a little laugh.

As the pen quivered in her shaking hands, she admitted to herself that she was always so malleable in his arms. He had a way of just rendering her senseless. Every time.

'Five years!' she snapped, scribbling her signature across all the indicated places. 'Five *years!*'

'And is that so awful?' he asked tenderly. 'Five years?'

Once she signed it, he scooped up the papers, and filed them into his brief case. As he walked towards the door, he turned back and said to Sequoia 'Thank you for a beautiful evening.' He put his brief case down, and walked back to her. 'Can I drive you home?'

She grabbed hold of the chair. Can I drive you home, only meant one thing. She did not want Ruben Hazelwood in her bed. Or did she?

When she hesitated, he reached over, and kissed her on the cheek.

'Sweet dreams.'

One moment he is turning her on like a volcano ready to explode, and then the next he is walking away. Sequoia was a melting pot of unstable, dangerous heat. *That was cruel, Ruben. Very cruel.* And she couldn't help but think that he was having the last laugh.

Table for Two?

The following Friday night, just as the big hand indicated six o-clock, the phone in *Treble Clef* rang; its shrill *tring tring tring* making Sequoia jump out of her skin.

'I'm afraid I can't make it to the café,' Ruben's voice rumbled down the phone line. 'I'm tied up in a meeting for another two hours. I'm sorry.'

Click. He hung up the phone. No hello Sequoia. No goodbye Sequoia. Since when did he become so rude?

Sequoia staggered to the table for two that she had set, and blew out the candle with fury. After all the darned fuss he'd made about the lease including weekly meetings, and he couldn't even make it to the first one! She laughed, then, ironically, at the thought of five years looming ahead of her. He didn't even have the ability to commit for one week! *Bored already, Ruben?* she wondered. *Did you get a better offer?*

Astonished at how dejected she felt, Sequoia trudged home along the sandy shoreline, when she happened upon Jack fishing up on the cove.

'Hey Jack,' she smiled warmly. Things had been different since the ball, she knew that, but she did like him, and still wanted to be friends. Sequoia wasn't ready to go home yet: she didn't need the reminder that Ruben had just stood her up.

Taming her wild thoughts, she reminded herself that it was not a date; it was a business arrangement. Jack soon had her forgetting the disappointment, and she found herself laughing softly at a story he regaled her with about five-year-old twins and their determination to leave his shop with no less than ten books. Jack had a soft spot for children, and in that moment she wondered if he'd ever be a father. Would he ever marry again? Her heart ached for him, and she wondered if this is what love really felt like. Was it about compassion and empathy rather than heat and lust? The feelings she had with Jack couldn't have been further removed from the ones she had whenever she was within shouting distance of Ruben.

In a simple moment of affection, she reached and wrapped her arm around his shoulders to let him know that there were no hard feelings; not from her side, anyway.

'If you ever change your mind, Sequoia, you know where I am,' he said softly, the wind carrying his words away on the breeze.

'I know that Jack. I know.' That was her cue to leave for she didn't want to go down this path with him again, nor did she want to keep bruising his heart with her near-misses. She picked up her shoes and backpack, and headed up the bank and onto the beachside road.

If she didn't know better, she'd have thought the black BMW speeding under the glow of street lights was Ruben, but it couldn't have been. He was in a business meeting. Wasn't he?

Adagio did her usual acrobatic flips, such was her delight at seeing Sequoia.

'Hungry girl, hey?' she said, scooping the ever-growing kitten into her arms and feeling the full joy of her purr.

It had been a long week at the café, and Sequoia wanted to soak in the bath and let go of all the tension and the frustration she felt at Ruben letting her down at the last minute. Why did she have to keep thinking about him?

Steamy water filled the bath while Sequoia lit three beeswax candles, and added some jasmine oil to the hot water. The clear vocals of Norah Jones sang through the speakers. Sequoia climbed into the deep tub of water, and sighed with relief at such simple pleasures. Thoughts turned to Ruben, and his thermal pool in Tuscany, and how each evening the hot water drugged her; made her weak. Finally, she allowed herself to relax, to let go of the long day. But Ruben was never far from her slumber-like thoughts, and she admitted to herself that it felt safer thinking about him when he wasn't standing in the same room.

Sequoia had probably been asleep for a few minutes when something woke her up with a start. Adagio meowed, and was scratching at the side of the bath. There, standing barefoot in the doorway, long and lean, and ever so gorgeous in faded denim jeans and a white skin-hugging t-shirt, was Ruben. Smiling.

Sequoia reached to cover herself with her hands, and snapped 'Oh my god, you could have given me a heart attack! You're trespassing. Don't you know how to knock?'

'I did.' And he just stood there, surveying the beauty before him.

'Can you please leave?'

'No.'

'Ruben!'

'I'm not going anywhere. We had an agreement to meet each Friday night. I was a bit late, that's all.'

'We didn't agree to meet in my bathroom, with me naked!'

'I always preferred you this way.'

Everything about her body language gave her feelings away.

'Shall I help you dry?' he asked, passing her a thick hot-pink towel. 'Or I could just take you as you are.'

'Ruben!'

'You know whenever you say my name like that it really turns me on,' and his smile had her body pulsating uncontrollably.

She was about to say, 'Ru...' and then realised it was better to shut her mouth.

Ruben reached over and helped her out of the bathtub. It was obvious that he was deeply aroused, and she hoped, she prayed, he couldn't tell that she felt the same way. 'Let me get dressed, and then I'll meet you in the kitchen for your darned business meeting!'

'No,' he said. 'I'm not leaving.'

'R...' and his hands were around her shoulders.

There would be no business meeting tonight.

The scent of jasmine oil lingered on her damp, warm skin, but she was so awake, so alive in her desire, that she was also aware of the sweet scent of her attraction to him.

As he pulled her close, and she felt him hard and strong against her bare belly. When she tried to say his name, Sequoia couldn't recognise her voice. The words were coming from some place new inside her. As he pressed himself against her, leaving Sequoia in no doubt what he wanted, of what they *both* wanted, he groaned as her hips moved towards him. Then he let her go and stripped off his shirt, his jeans, his briefs.

Whisking Sequoia off her feet, Ruben heard the roll from her throat of primal pleasure. There was no shame on her face. No guilt. No *inexperience*. Sequoia was a woman who *wanted*.

'Tell me you're not thinking of Jack Breardon now.'

'What?' she murmured, barely able to think.

'Who do you want Sequoia? Me or Jack?'

She looked up at him, astonished.

'I saw you with your arms around him on the beach earlier,' his menacing in her ear. 'Who do you want?' he asked her one more time.

'You, Ruben. It's only ever been...' It had been too long, way too long since she'd made love to a man. To *Ruben*.

She couldn't speak, but her whole body told him the answer with a delicious, involuntary quiver. He played to her mood, and she to his.

'Tell me again, Sequoia, do you want me?' His mouth reached down, and he buried his stubble-covered chin into her neck.

Fire doesn't exist in its natural form, they discovered, and only by consuming each other could it come into being. They were on fire. Fireworks shot out across the bay.

Grieving Hearts

It was the bleaching sunshine upon her face which woke Sequoia at first light the next morning. Afterr rubbing her eyes, she rolled back into the sheets, whispering Ruben's name, determined not to come out of the dream she was in: Ruben was in her bed, making love to her, here, in this house. Such a beautifully erotic dream. As she awoke fully, she realised the truth: Oh yes, Ruben had been here. Her breath was ragged and her pulse pumping.

Flashes of memory about Jack on the beach played at the edges of her mind, but everything about Ruben had been a dream. A perfect dream: Him standing, so ruggedly handsome, in her bathroom then whisking her off to bed.

Sequoia looked around the room. Where was he? She tiptoed to the kitchen. Naked. Not in the kitchen, not in the bathroom. Then she peeped out the front window. No sign of his car. Odd. Maybe it was a dream?

Glancing at the kitchen clock, she realised she only had half an hour to get into the café. Saturdays were busy, so there was no point in moping around. Perhaps she'd call him later.

The steam of the shower was a pertinent souvenir of the previous night. Sequoia had never known such heat, even all those years ago. As she let her hands caress her body, she reminisced at his deft touch. How could she still be so exquisitely sensitive to his touch?

It was going to be a long day at work! The last thing she wanted to do today was cook; she wanted to go back to bed. With Ruben.

Standing in front of her wardrobe, surveying the clothes, she dismissed her trademark denim jeans. Today, she wanted to dress like a woman who'd been well loved. It wasn't wholly appropriate for a day in the kitchen, but she didn't care. Slipping into a flattering, red jersey, wrap-around dress, which emphasised her breasts and hips, she admired herself in the mirror, and then stepped into matching sandals. Dabbing on a few drops of essential oil of jasmine: the same drops she'd sprinkled into last night's bath, she nearly felt herself explode with the memory of where Ruben had taken her in the small hours of the night.

It was such a beautiful day that Sequoia decided against driving the short distance to *Treble Clef*, and instead walked the beachside road. She'd never felt so alive, so liberated, so *touched*. It was as if every cell in her body was singing. And more than anything, she couldn't wait to see Ruben again. If there was time, she'd call him during a lull at work.

Ali had arrived at work before her, and was sautéing onions for the carrot and ginger soup.

Sequoia floated in on a breeze, her deliriousness on the verge of irritating Ali.

As Sequoia mixed the lemon and coconut dough, she breathed in the fresh citrus scent with over-enthusiastic pleasure. 'These smell so delicious.'

'You're crazy,' Ali laughed out loud. 'Just make the biscuits already.'

Sequoia laughed.

'But they smell so good!' she insisted.

'From the look on your face this morning, the whole world is going to smell good. God help any man who walks through that door this morning. By the way, which man is responsible for this?'

Sequoia raised a mischievous eyebrow. 'Nooooooooooooo?' Ali asked disbelievingly. 'Ruben? Not the infamous love rat? How on Earth did he get you into his bed?'

'It was *my* bed, actually.'

Ali shook her head, and they were interrupted by the front door bell ringing as the first of the day's customers made their way into *Treble Clef.*

Sequoia surveyed her café: her pride and pleasure. Wood featured strongly in the design, boasting Tasmania's Huon pine, lending its honey-bold colouring to the seats, counters and window seats. She smiled at the thought that Ruben had also been taken with such a beautiful natural resource, and had used it extensively in the hotel.

The front windows and veranda afforded fabulous views of the bay. It had the added bonus of advertising what a great café it was to anyone who walked by. They were magnetically drawn in.

Outside the front door was a covered porch area, which featured seating for 20 diners. Horse riders often tied up their animal to one of the four porch posts while they sipped coffee.

Treble Clef was a thirty-second walk from the beach on the other side of the road. On each table, Sequoia placed vases with fresh flowers, and a small white lantern.

In the far corner of the café stood a baby-grand piano, and several large tropical house plants. A CD played a mix of modern country music. On the wide front counter was a selection of the day's cakes: passionfruit and coconut, triple chocolate, vanilla and raspberry sponge, and carrot and pineapple.

A party of three settled themselves into the corner table, giggling about a movie they'd seen the night before. Sequoia bought them lattes and peppermint tea, and a trio of cheese and chive scones with a serving of marmalade.

Jack came in through the door. Sequoia could immediately tell something was wrong. She flinched inside, wondering if he knew about her and Ruben. Don't be silly, he couldn't possibly know. Was she feeling guilty? Yes, guilt. One minute she was on the beach rejecting Jack, and within a short time was experiencing the dizzying heights of lovemaking with Ruben. Of course she felt guilty.

Jack's eyes were bloodshot.

'Jack, whatever is the matter? You don't look well at all,' she said softly, so as not to draw attention to him.

Without warning, he sobbed, and then spluttered out that his mother had just been killed in a car accident in Queensland. The news came through only an hour ago. A policeman had turned up at the bookshop to inform him. 'I'm flying to the mainland this afternoon to formally identify her body.'

Sequoia instinctively wrapped her arms around him. The pain, agony and heartbreak of losing your mother was something she knew too well. But for Jack to lose her like this, without warning? No chance to say goodbye? Sequoia could only begin to imagine the horror.

As she let him settle into her arms, she only looked up slightly when the front door opened. The ring of the string of Tibetan bells was their way of knowing a customer had entered.

Ruben's body filled the height of the doorway. As he stood stock still, Sequoia looked on helplessly as pain clawed down his face. Sequoia wanted to run to him, to explain that this embrace wasn't what it looked like; that Jack's head nestled into her neck wasn't a passionate kiss. What could she do? What should she do? She was torn. Torn between chasing after Ruben as he strode furiously down the pavement, and staying with Jack in his moment of need. Sequoia chose Jack. Ruben could learn the truth later. Jack's needs couldn't wait.

Ali looked at the scene which played out before her, eyes wide in disbelief at the timing, and marvelled at Sequoia's resilience and steadfastness to another human's pain. *That* was the Sequoia she knew and loved. No wonder she was the Bay's surrogate agony aunt for love-struck teenagers and other wayward souls! Hers was a gentle touch; she had a reverence for other people's tender hearts.

Sequoia packed up a basket of food for Jack to take, and walked him down to the carpark. As he climbed into the driver's seat, he looked up and said 'Thank you for being there Sequoia. It means the world to me. It really does.'

'Where else could I have been, Jack?' And though her heart screamed that she wanted to be with Ruben, she knew that there were times in life when you had to put someone else's needs ahead of your own, regardless of the cost. But surely there was no cost? There couldn't be. Not after last night.

When she returned to *Treble Clef*, she phoned Hazelwood Hotel.

'May I speak to Ruben please, it's Sequoia Lissen.'

The phone rang through on another line, and

101

then the receptionist returned and said 'I'm afraid Mr Hazelwood is in a meeting. May I take a message?'

'Yes, please ask him to call me as soon as he can.'

When she returned from a brisk walk on the beach just after lunch, she asked Ali if he'd phoned.

'Nope. Perhaps you should try him again?'

Several times throughout the afternoon she phoned, always leaving a message. And Sequoia did the same again the next day from home. It was the longest Sunday she'd ever experienced in her life.

The number of times she phoned each day began to dwindle. Well, she consoled herself, she'd see him on Friday night.

Friday brought with it a chill wind, and the day soon came and went. Sequoia prepared Ruben one of his favourite meals: Wild mushrooms and dill in a filo wrap with cranberry and orange sauce. By 11pm she accepted that he wasn't going to turn up for their weekly meeting.

Sequoia stopped calling the hotel. And she stopped looking at the front door or her answering machine expectantly.

Ruben had assumed the worst of her when he saw her arms around Jack. The *worst*. How could he, after the night they'd shared?

When the following Friday night came and went with no sign of him, she decided there was nothing for it but to drive over to Hazelwood Hotel and confront him.

'I'm here to see Ruben Hazelwood,' she told the receptionist.

'He's overseas at the moment. But,' she said, looking in his diary, 'He's due back in tomorrow. Can I take a message?' she asked far too chirpily for Sequoia's liking.

'Overseas? What's he doing overseas? Where is he?' she demanded.

'He's not there on business, so it's actually none of my business, but his solicitor, Hannah Harman, did let it slip that he was going to the U.S.A on a personal matter. She said something about it being a matter that was close to his heart. I don't know what that means. I'm sorry,' she confided.

Two weeks later, and there was still no sign of him. Sequoia decided to play him at his own game, and made an appointment with her solicitor.

'He's breached this contract. We're meant to meet each Friday night!' she said, shaking the contract in the air as if it might just change the world.

Tom Brown read through the document, looked up at her and lowered his reading glasses down his nose a little.

'Actually, it says you need to be available each Friday night. It doesn't actually say he needs to be there. I'm sorry Sequoia.'

Confused and furious, she stormed out of the office. What was Ruben playing at? If he wasn't going to return her calls, then she'd go back to the hotel and see him.

'I'm afraid Mr Hazelwood doesn't work from here anymore. May I fetch the managing director for you?' the young woman asked helpfully.

'No. I want to see Ruben. Where is he? Where can I find him?'

'I'm not supposed to give out his home address. That's where he works from. It's against company policy, and he has strict rules about privacy.'

'I'll bet he does! I'll give you a month of free lunches at *Treble Clef* if you tell me where he is. Please? Even the street name is enough.'

'That's very generous, Miss Lissen. But it's not necessary. Look, if you head up to Hazards Mountain Road and just happen to see a black convertible BMW then you might be in the right area. Assuming it's in the driveway, that is. If it was inside the garage, you'd probably have to be guided by the strip of young cypress trees on the front lawn.'

'Thank you,' Sequoia said sincerely, squeezing the receptionist's hand. 'I won't tell a soul.'

Sequoia wasn't sure her violet-coloured VW beetle would make it up the mountain road, but both she and the car persevered. The view! Never before had she been this far up the hills. It was stunning. When she pulled up in front of Ruben's house, she didn't need a car or the view to say it was his; the design alone whispered his name across the sea breeze. His ability to create a building which enhanced the landscape rather than blotted it was truly something to be admired. Not today though. Today she had other things to think about besides admiring his genius.

Palpitations nearly immobilised her as she walked across the immaculate lawn but she was determined to tell Ruben that what he'd witnessed between her and Jack was nothing more than a show of genuine empathy.

Knock, knock, knock. Sequoia could have used the doorbell, but she wanted to touch his front door; needed to feel she was connecting with him before their eyes met. That beautiful wooden door was opened by an even more beautiful woman: lithe, tall, blonde and looked like she'd stepped off a photo shoot for Californian beachwear. 'May I help you,' she drawled in a broad New York accent.

Sequoia apologised, saying that she must be at the wrong house.

Ruben approached the door.

'Hannah, that will be all for today. I'll see you next week.'

The woman collected her brief case, returned to the front door and squeezed past Sequoia with a huge smile wrapped across her face. With the sleekness of a feline on heat, she sauntered to her red sports car. Sequoia hadn't even paid much attention to it, assuming it was just another of Ruben's toys.

'My solicitor,' he said curtly, as if to justify the woman's presence, then ushered her inside.

Sequoia looked around the vast open-plan room. It was tastefully decorated as much for style as for comfort. Wide floorboards, polished with beeswax, were one of the main features. That, and the million-dollar view.

'Really looks like a solicitor,' Sequoia muttered as she spied the two empty champagne glasses. Her blood began to boil. 'Doesn't look like a business meeting either!'

'Who said it was a business meeting?' he snarled, and then asked gruffly, 'What do you want?'

'You haven't returned my phone calls. I've only left about 64 of them. You've missed our Friday meetings.'

Ruben didn't answer, but sat down on one of the large white sofas, picking up some paperwork.

'And?' he said, sounding more than a little bored.

'You came into my home and made love to me until I was senseless, and then....then you cut me off. It's cruel!'

Ruben put down the papers, and looked her in the eyes.

'I made love to you because I thought that's what you wanted, but within hours—*hours*—of leaving your bed, I find you in the arms of another man! Don't talk to me about *cruel*. You didn't want me Sequoia. You just wanted a body. Someone to scratch an itch.'

If Ruben had kicked her in the stomach, it would have hurt less.

'You can go now,' he said, as if dismissing a staff member.

'No!' she said, hands on hips. 'No! I will not go until you hear me out! Jack's mother had just been killed in a car accident. Just an hour before you walked into the café. I was holding him because he was grieving!'

'Sequoia,' he interrupted, about to apologise, but she tore into him so fast and furiously, that he decided to keep his mouth closed.

'Grief hurts, Ruben! It's excruciatingly painful. It rips your soul apart. You've clearly never lost anyone close to you, or you wouldn't be so heartless.'

'Sequoia...'

'You! You're so damn arrogant you think there's only one reason why a woman touches a man. You're right Ruben. I don't want you. I don't know what I was thinking coming here today. I'm pulling out of the contract. All of it. I'm leaving Coles Bay. You've ruined everything about this place for me. Keeping *Treble Clef* is too high a price to pay to be anywhere near you!'

'Don't be so impulsive Sequoia. Don't throw away your café. I lived here for three years without you being

106

any the wiser. I'm sure we can just get on with our lives and never see each other again. After all,' he said, running his tired fingers through his dark hair, 'it's not like our worlds mix' he said, and then walked to the large window with his back to her.

Sequoia stood still, speechless. What sort of game was he playing?

'Haven't you hurt me enough, Ruben? Why do you have to keep doing this?'

'As I said, you can go now.'

Sequoia was tempted to scream so loudly that the whole of Coles Bay would hear. Frantically she searched for words to penetrate his rigid heart, and as if reading her thoughts he said 'Don't say anything you might regret Sequoia. It's hard to take words back when they've been spoken in anger.'

'Regret?' she shrieked, completely incensed. 'I regret the day you walked into my life. I regret letting you sweep me off my vulnerable, grief-stricken feet. I regret *you!*'

'Sequoia,' he said calmly, as he turned around, slowly.

His eyes followed every inch of her body, looking her up and down, taking her in, memorising her in case he never saw her again. 'Goodbye.'

Unable to move, she felt herself frozen in time. Was this really happening?

'Damn it, can you leave now?' he asked impatiently.

Sequoia walked up to him and was so close to his face that she couldn't tell that he was tormented by her beauty, vulnerability, volatility and desperation.

'I loved you. You became my whole world,' she said as her fists pounded against his chest in a rage. Not once did he try to stop her.

'I loved you!' she sobbed. 'And I know you loved me. I know you did. I saw the ring. I saw the card...' Eight years of pain thumped right into his chest, but still he didn't wrap his arms around her.

Sequoia was unaware that Ruben was fighting every instinct so he could remain detached: just like he'd been taught his entire life. Nor did she know that what he really wanted to do was hold her, to never let her go; but he turned away. She would never know that he turned so she couldn't see his tears.

'Young, fat and stupid. Yep, that's what the media said. And *you* let them. Well I'll tell you something Ruben Hazelwood. I'm none of those now. None. Look at me!'

He stood still, his fists clenched, his back to her.

'You can't promise someone forever and then just change your mind. Ruben!'

And still he didn't move.

'I don't ever want to say goodbye to you again. I couldn't deal with it. If you let me walk out this door then I will *never* come back. Do you hear me?'

All she could see was his back. She had no way of knowing that his eyes were searching out to sea, and that they were filled with more salty tears than Coles Bay could ever hold. Perhaps if she thought a little more about his past she'd know that there was only one thing stopping him from turning around and conceding that he was wrong. One thing: pride. Good old-fashioned Hazelwood pride. And that his father's words haunted him. 'Stiff upper lip, boy'; 'Boys don't cry'. 'We're English. We're dignified. Think with your head, not your heart.'

How could he think, for even a moment, that she'd run to Jack's arms after the night they'd shared? Why was he was acting like a jealous lover, when there was nothing— absolutely nothing—to be jealous of.

'I see,' she said bitterly. 'You've got another woman in your bed now to keep you warm. That's all I ever was to you, wasn't I? A warm body.'

There was no fight left in her, and so she ran from the room, almost sidelined by the grand piano to one side. Despite the torment scratching at her soul, she couldn't understand why he owned a piano. It wasn't as if he could play. Just one more thing to spend his money on! At speed, she headed out across the lawn to her car. It was all she could do not to vomit when she saw Malibu Barbie in her red car, chatting away on her mobile phone while simultaneously touching up her siren-red lipstick.

As Sequoia drove away, she saw the blonde step out of her car and walk back into Ruben's house.

All the way down the mountain Sequoia screamed, her words lost in the wind. Regrets? Driving away, leaving him to the Barbie doll, was the biggest regret of all.

Food Poisoning

The next few weeks passed in a blur. Sequoia had to admit she was thoroughly miserable. The only thing she wanted was Ruben back in her life, and now there was no chance of them getting back together. As each day went on, she felt less like her happy self. Her diary included aromatherapy massages, playing tennis with Ali on Sunday afternoons, buying a bunch of books from Jack's shop, gym workouts, and even sewing a whole new selection of blouses, but nothing, nothing at all, eased the discontent. Eventually she started going off her food, too upset to eat; and her usual joy in preparing food for *Treble Clef* began to wane.

When Sequoia left France, she'd been devastated, but even then she still ate a little. These days, nothing appealed to her.

As she peeled the potatoes for the cauliflower and potato gratin on today's menu, Sequoia felt an odd shift in her belly. And without another thought, raced into the staff toilet and threw up. When she emerged a few minutes later, Ali said 'You look like death. Have you caught a bug?'

White, unsteady on her feet, and hands shaking, Sequoia said 'I must have.'

'Go home. I'll have to manage on my own. Can't have that around here. Go.'

Sequoia stumbled to her car, grateful she'd driven down this morning rather than walked. There in the driver's seat, she tried to calm herself down. The smell of the leather interior made her convulse, and she heaved onto the asphalt car park. Grabbing a tissue from her pocket, she wiped her lips.

'Oh God,' she moaned, and then drove home slowly. Try as she might, Sequoia couldn't remember the last time she'd felt so ill.

Once home, she crawled into bed and cried. Adagio scratched at the bedroom door, desperate to be let in. Sequoia had been feeling a bit under the weather since her visit to Ruben's house, and his complete rejection of her. Perhaps this was a delayed reaction? A type of post traumatic stress disorder? It had been traumatic; there was no arguing with that! But maybe it was food poisoning? She mentally scanned through all her food prep, double checking everything had been done correctly.

For the first time in years, Sequoia really missed her mother, and started to cry for her. She needed her love, her arms, and her kind words. More than anything, she wanted some tender nurturing and wholesome advice.

Four days later, Ali said over the phone 'This is some nasty bug. Better get yourself to the doctor. I'll make an appointment for you, and call you back.'

'Thanks, Ali.' Sequoia sank back into her bed, grateful for her friend's kindness.

In less than a week, she'd lost half a stone. The thought of food made her feel so ill. Passing away the hours in bed, she'd tried imagining recipes she could create when she returned to the café, but that was always a bad idea. Every single image of food had her retching over the sick bowl.

How was she going to get to the doctor? She was in no state to drive. After calling a taxi, Sequoia threw on a t-shirt, cardigan and leggings, and bunched her hair under a sports cap. *I don't smell good*, she moaned.

'Sequoia?' Dr Charles greeted her. 'This is an honour. I never get to see you. I was starting to take it personally,' he chuckled, and passed her a bowl just in time.

'I'm so sorry,' she said, accepting a tissue.

'How long have you had this bug?'

'About a week now. At first, I wasn't vomiting. Just a bit under the weather, you know. Nothing I could put my finger on.'

'Okay, and are you sick all day long? Are you sick at night?' he asked, writing down notes.

'No, my tummy usually feels more settled at night.'

'When was your last menstrual period?' he asked matter of factly, rather than if it was a life-changing question.

'My period?' she repeated, looking up at him. What a stupid question. 'My last *menstrual* period?' Sequoia did some maths, and said. 'I don't know. Um, six or seven weeks ago. Maybe. Aggggh.'

She retched again.

'I can't be,' she insisted.

'Have you done a pregnancy test?' he asked.

'Er, no. No I haven't. You must think I'm *really* stupid?' she said, crimson cheeked and flustered.

'No, I think you've probably got a lot on your plate. Here,' he said, passing her a small packet. 'Take this into the toilet over there, and pee onto it. We'll soon find out if you're going to be a mummy.'

Mummy?

It was not a word she'd ever associated with herself. Raised as an only child by a single mother, she was sure that it was not a road she'd ever go down. No. Being a parent, for her, meant being in a loving family, with a devoted father and husband. It would go against everything she knew to bring a child into this world who would spend years of its life longing for a father. Tears swelled in her eyes, and she took out the pregnancy stick to pee on. Slowly. Like time was standing still, the lines changed colour. Oh My God. Her heart, thumping right through her body, raced like an express train.

'I'm pregnant?'

It was incomprehensible to her. They'd only made love once. Well, three times, but it was all on the same night!

Unlike her mother, she knew the surname of her baby's father. Ruben made it quite clear that he didn't want to be in her life. After all, he let her walk away. There was no going back. This firmed up her decision to leave Coles Bay. If Ruben got wind of this baby, there'd be no telling what he'd make her do, or if he'd try to buy the baby to continue the Hazelwood dynasty.

No, she had to break the lease agreement and move on.

The doctor realised the shock was crippling her, and offered to drive her home. 'Thanks, but I'll be fine. I'll get a taxi back.'

'I'll take a blood test while you're here,' he said, preparing the needle. 'Come back in a couple of weeks and we'll talk about finding you a midwife. In the meantime, here's some literature.'

Afterwards, she stumbled out of his room and into the reception area of the surgery. At no level did she feel ready to walk out into the bright sunshine. Sequoia breathed in deeply.

'May I phone a taxi?' she asked the receptionist.

'Sure, here's the number,' the middle-aged woman said, passing her a business card and the phone.

Sequoia sat down for a few minutes, digesting the u-turn her life was about to take. *Breathe, girl, breathe,* she repeated like a sacred mantra. She couldn't have been more shocked if someone had held her at gunpoint.

'Of course people get pregnant from having sex! What was I thinking?' she asked herself. And a laughing voice inside her head said 'You weren't thinking!'

I should have known better from my mother's example.

Spying the taxi through the surgery window, she stepped out and flinched from the harsh sunlight. Her only thought was to get back to bed. Fast. As she stepped onto the footpath, a hand caught her elbow.

'Are you okay, Sequoia?' Ruben asked, concern betraying the harsh man she'd not spoken to in weeks.

'As if you care!' she spat. 'I'm fine. Let me go.' She tried pulling away.

He placed a hand either side of her waist to steady her, and to look firmly into her eyes.

'Are you unwell?'

'A bug. Stay away so you don't catch it,' she murmured. 'Got a taxi waiting. Can't chat,' but as she waved him off and turned away she didn't see that he caught the words *So You're Pregnant* on the brochure in her hand.

Ruben instantly knew it was their baby, and that she hadn't been, and wouldn't be, with any other man. All at once he wanted to dance a jig, to shout it across the bay, but that she just walked away and didn't tell him that they were having a baby felt like a kick in the guts. Ruben shook his head. Sequoia had every right to walk away, and he deserved it. He should *never* have let her walk away. Ruben watched the taxi pull away, and his hands began to shake. How could he make things right? There was no way that she was raising their baby on her own, and he had to make amends because he didn't want to spend another day apart from her.

Ruben followed the taxi to her home, and knocked on the door.

'Let me in Sequoia. Let me look after you.' After knocking solidly for an hour, his knuckles began to bleed. Ruben had knocked on the front door, back door, bedroom door, kitchen window, and bathroom window. If only there was a way inside. There was nothing for it, he decided. To hell with being a gentleman!

'Sequoia, if you don't answer this door right now I'm going to break it down. Let me in.'

Slowly, ever so slowly, it creaked open. Sequoia looked up at him, terrified and sick.

'Let me look after you.' Ruben walked in, picked her up off her feet and carried her to bed. 'This is *our* baby. You're not alone,' he whispered in to her ear.

'How do you know?' she gasped.

'The brochure in your hands.'

'I don't need you. I'm doing this on my own. I don't know what I'm doing, I haven't made any concrete decisions,' she lied. 'But I do know this, Ruben: I don't need your help, your pity, your money, your advice. If my mother could raise a child on her own, then I damn well can!'

'Calm down. You're not your mother. This situation is completely different. Your mum didn't even know your dad's surname. You *do* know my name. And,' he brushed the loose hair from the side of her cheek 'And you know I love you.'

And there, for the first time in eight years, Ruben Hazelwood had said it out loud.

'How can I ever believe you? You couldn't say

it before, when I really needed to hear it. And now, frankly, Ruben I don't need to hear it anymore than I need you. You made your choice. You let me walk away. Why? So you could have a bit of fun with the blonde brains?'

'She's my solicitor.'

'A solicitor who sips champagne in business hours? Please!' She turned away from him, and reached for her sick bowl. Ruben rubbed her back, and pulled a clean handkerchief from his pocket.

'Let me clean you up in the shower,' he said gently.

'I hope you're kidding.'

It had been days since she'd showered, and Sequoia knew she didn't look or smell good.

'I can look after myself,' she snapped.

'Yeah, I can see that,' he said, and lifting her off the bed walked her into the shower. Turning on the taps so that the pressure was at full speed, he began to undress her. She'd no sooner stepped into the shower than she blushed as he dispersed with his suit, shirt, tie, shoes, socks, briefs. And despite how unwell she felt, and how she'd just spoken to him, he was so aroused by being this close to her that she couldn't bear to look at him.

With great tenderness and care, Ruben washed her hair, and rubbed her back. Then his hands went to her belly, and he held her close. As much as he wanted to, he wouldn't make love to her now, at least not in that way.

'I love you, Sequoia. I have never stopped loving you.'

'No Ruben. You've hurt me too many times. I can't do this. Stop messing with my mind.'

Instead, he let his hands speak. Softly caressing every square inch of her body, he brought pleasure to her in ways that she didn't think were possible.

Putty in his hands, again! And so, after the shower, once he'd changed the sheets and pillow cases, she let him tuck her into bed. Ruben kissed her softly on the forehead, then lay beside her; both of them naked, wrapped in each other's arms as they fell asleep.

In the morning, Sequoia woke up before him. As she watched him sleeping, her heart ached. Determined to raise this baby on her own, she figured that he'd just have to deal with it.

When Ruben awoke, he reached over to her and said 'I'm taking you to my house until you're better. And Sequoia, don't argue.' Without answering back, she watched him as he stepped out of bed, showered, fed the cat, then came back and said 'Don't worry, the kitten is coming with us.'

Sequoia sighed. At this point, she was too unwell to argue. So much for pregnancy being a time that made women blossom. She was wilting!

Ruben held her hand, and guided her to his car. Adagio was in a box on the back seat, mewling.

Nurtured

It felt odd to be back in Ruben's palatial mansion. More than once she'd marvelled at his ability to take wealth and make it personal.

Sequoia didn't argue when Ruben made her comfortable on one of the sofas where she could have a view over Coles Bay and beyond.

'I won't be long. Let me get a room ready for you,' he said.

Sequoia pulled the blanket above her shoulders, and Adagio settled into her lap.

The sight of the piano, once again, unsettled her. It still didn't make sense why he'd own a top-of-the-range instrument, the price of which made her eyes water, when he wasn't a pianist. When it came to his home life, Ruben was a hermit, and didn't entertain, so there was no logical explanation.

'Ruben?' she said, when he returned to the room, 'Why do you have a piano? And, let's face it, it's not just any piano. My fingers tremble at the thought of ever playing something like that! Why?'

Looking at her for the longest time, he said softly 'I bought it so you could play for me on my birthday.' And without another word, he left the room again.

Birthday. Birthday? She was trying to remember, and then her heart sank. Of course she remembered when his birthday was! A lump formed in her throat. Here he was looking after her every waking need, and all she'd done was fob him off when he had wanted some musical pleasure. His birthday had been the day after the Ball of the Bay, and he clearly expected the evening to end somewhat differently. She hadn't even registered that it had been his birthday. It was only, now, by remembering that it was on his birthday that they'd met, all those years ago in France, that she was able to put the pieces together.

'Just need to pop out for a few minutes,' he said casually, as he waved goodbye. And within a minute she heard the motor of his car starting up in the driveway.

Looking at the mountains, the bay and the small town below, Sequoia wondered what a man like Ruben was doing in a place like this, so far off the beaten track. Surely he'd be happier in the city, with butlers, maids and a concierge at his beck and call?

Tiredness overcame her, and she drifted off into peaceful slumber. Just her and Adagio. Half an hour later, she was awoken by the sound of keys in the front door. Sequoia looked up, expecting to see Ruben, but instead saw a lady dressed in a black and white uniform.

'Hello dear, I'm just here to clean the house. I don't normally come in on Tuesdays, but Ruben has asked me to straighten things up a bit. I won't be in your way.'

Sequoia chuckled. 'Straighten things up? There's nothing to straighten up.'

'Ruben can see a speck of dust from a mile away. He likes things *just so*,' the elderly lady smiled back. "*Just so*" she repeated, so Sequoia got the message. 'Can I get you anything to eat or drink while I'm here?'

'No, I'm fine, thanks.' Sequoia said, closing her eyes again, and wondering how Mr OCD coped in her home, with her piles of cookery and gardening magazines scattered carelessly around the living room and bedroom: her empty coffee cups lined on the bedside table. Not once had he said a word about them, and hadn't even raised an eyebrow.

'My name's Marion, by the way. Just shout if there's anything you need.'

'Thanks Marion.'

When Ruben returned, he said to Sequoia, 'Time for you to go to bed, I think.' And he scooped her up in his arms, and carried her down the hallway. 'You should be comfortable in here,' he said warmly.

Surveying the room, she immediately realised it was his bedroom. Were they going to sleep together? She'd assumed he'd put her into a guest room.

When the shock settled, Sequoia noticed several vases filled with beautiful flowers: hot-pink gerberas, Singapore orchids, Blue Moon roses, red lilies. There was a pile of reading material by the bedside, a large glass pitcher of water, with a single slice of lemon floating inside, and a bowl of fruit: grapes, peaches, nectarines, and strawberries.

'Wow, this is first-class care.'

'For a first-class lady,' was all Ruben said.

'It's morning sickness, Ruben, I'm not dying. You really didn't have to do this.' She was already feeling guilty. As soon as she was better and back on her feet, she'd be breaking the news to him.

By day, she slept, read, and picked at the fruit. The view from the bedroom was of the mountains, and she found it deeply nourishing to not have to think about anything but herself...*and their baby*. Ali had help in the café so that was a major worry off her mind.

At night, Ruben lay beside her, his hand gently over her belly. Not once did he approach her to make love, though she knew, just knew, that he'd have bought the Moon to touch her in that way; she marvelled at his restraint.

Late Friday afternoon, a knock on the bedroom door woke Sequoia from a nap.

'Honey, there's someone here to see you,' Ruben said, ushering the lady in. 'This is Sarah. She'll be your independent midwife.'

'Hi Sarah,' Sequoia said, scooching herself up in bed. 'Sorry, I'd have dressed if I'd known I was having company.'

'Don't worry about that!' she laughed, and Sequoia immediately warmed to her. The midwife was in her twenties, about the same age as Sequoia, and wore her hair in two long blonde plaits. 'So, you've not been too well then? It should pass in the couple of weeks, and then you'll feel amazing and wonder what all the fuss was about.'

Sequoia appreciated how relaxed Sarah was, and how she made her feel. Ruben perched at the end of the bed, taking in every word.

'So, this is your first pregnancy?' Sarah asked, taking notes.

'Yes.'

'And do you know what your mother's pregnancy was like when she was carrying you?'

It seemed like such an odd question, and to have her mother here, right now, in the room with them in this way, took her by surprise.

Ruben immediately picked up on it, and moved to her side of the bed, and held her hand.

'Mum had a straightforward pregnancy, and birth was quick and simple. A midwife attended the birth, and mum breastfed me with ease. It was a typical New Age hippy birth in California: waterbirth, candles, chanting,' she laughed, 'No complications at all.'

'That's great. It's always nice to have a straightforward history,' Sarah said, writing it all down.

'Did the doctor talk about your birth options with you?'

'I'm afraid I was in too much shock to think about anything other than how to stop being sick!' Sequoia laughed.

'Okay, well, you can go down the hospital route, which is what a lot of women do, or you can have a midwife attend you at home or at a birthing centre.'

'Could you come to my home, then?' Sequoia asked, drawn to the idea of birthing in private.

'Yes, absolutely,' Sarah said. 'Have you thought about if you'd like a waterbirth like your mum did, or to use hypnobirthing...'

'I haven't thought about anything!' Sequoia said. 'This has all happened so quickly. I'm still getting used to the idea that I've got a baby inside but I will think about all these ideas. Thank you.'

'The main thing right now is that you look after yourself, and I see Ruben is making sure you're well cared for,' she said, taking in the sight of all the flowers. 'Rest, eat well, and try and keep stress out of your life. The baby's going to grow and your job is to be a happy container. Do you think you can do that?' Sarah smiled, reaching out her hand.

'Yes,' she said, and she could feel Ruben's hand on one side, and Sarah's on the other. At that moment, she felt like she could handle anything.

'I've got a copy of your blood test results from the doctor. I don't think there's anything else I need right now, apart from checking your pulse and measurements. I'll come back and visit in a few weeks. By six months, I'll visit you each week.' Sarah said, packing up her bag.

'No stress!' she said, her laughter carrying though the air as she walked out of the room.

Ruben led her to the front door, and when he returned Sequoia said, 'I really like her. How much does she cost?'

'That's not a concern of yours Sequoia. I want you to have the best antenatal support you can get.' And just his tone made it quite clear that it wasn't up for discussion or negotiation. But Sequoia couldn't help wonder how she would maintain that level of care once she'd left Ruben's house. In her mind, she started playing with the idea of an independent midwife, and birthing in the privacy of her own home. Yes, she'd like that. How lovely, she decided, to give birth in a pool of warm water, with the hands of a midwife for support.

'Hungry?' Ruben asked, interrupting her as she developed a birth plan in her mind.

'I'm a bit peckish, actually,' she admitted.

'I'll get some dinner sorted. What do you feel like?' he asked, as if taking an order at a restaurant.

'Something quite simple: fresh vegetables, no heavy sauces or spices.'

'About an hour from now okay?'

'Perfect.'

A little later he came into the bedroom and asked if she was up to dining in the front room.

'I think so,' she said, climbing out of bed.

Dressed in a simple ivory-coloured broderie anglaise nightie Ruben had bought for her, she followed him into the living room.

Her heart softened at the table for two, lit up with candles and red roses. Norah Jones was playing on the stereo.

'This is lovely Ruben, but you really didn't have to go this effort.'

'It was no effort. No effort at all.'

Sequoia picked at the salad before her: rocket, mizuna, baby spinach leaves, and nestled on top were chargrilled artichokes, olives, cherry tomatoes and finely grated beetroot. Before long, she put down her fork and used her fingers to eat. Ruben stifled a laugh.

Sequoia licked her fingers slowly, her eyes closing as if she was enjoying sex rather than eating food.

'Oh this tastes so good. Food, I have missed you!' she laughed out loud.

'Don't overeat and make yourself sick,' he warned. 'I've never seen anyone eat a tomato so seductively!'

'Are you okay?' she asked, catching the change in his body language.

'Perfect. Just perfect.'

They ate their meal, with much laughter inbetween bites. Sequoia was grateful not to be feeling like a patient for the first time in a couple of weeks.

Afterwards, Ruben asked, 'Dance with me?' And she followed his lead.

Barefoot on the wooden floorboards, they slow-danced to *Come Away With Me*.

It felt like heaven to be in his arms, in this way, being loved into wholeness. An inner battle took place: she didn't want to leave his arms, not ever, but what choice did she have? Sequoia knew one thing: she had to get better. Every day that she stayed here, in his world where anything could be rustled up with the click of his fingers, made it all the harder to say goodbye.

As he gently sang the lyrics to her, she could feel, against the soft fabric of her nightie, exactly what he wanted to share with her. What he wanted to give to her.

Tears slipped from her eyes. How dare he lull her into the comfort and safety of this world, this manufactured world, so that she would find it impossible to tear herself away? But for now, she told herself, *just for now, get yourself well. And when you're feeling better and strong, then you can run. You know how to run. You've done it before.*

Tiredness overcame her. 'I need to go back to bed. Come away with me in the night,' she said, repeating the lyrics of the song they'd just danced to.

Ruben needed no encouragement. Without hesitation, he raised her off her feet, and delivered her to their bed. *Their* bed. And he slowly lifted off her nightie. His clothes followed them, a pile of fabric crumpled on the floor. *Just so.*

Sequoia felt his hands warming her and caressing each weary and tired part of her body. Kisses, soft as Summer rain, danced upon her skin, and she melted, falling, falling, falling. The only place she was running away to tonight was into sweet oblivion. There was no rush, no urgency, and no desperation to reach nirvana.

Ruben had never made love so slowly in his life.

They held each other for hours, not saying a word: just looking into each other's watery eyes. What were words anyway? They could never describe the intensity between them; the power, the volcanic eruptions of pleasure that soared through their veins.

The next morning, at about 10am, Ruben woke her with a whisper.

'I've got to go down to the hotel for a business meeting. I'll be back after lunch. I've fed the kitten, and there was a message from Ali to say she'd pop by briefly after work.'

125

Sequoia was barely awake, but she heard him. Her body was still warm and glowing. A business meeting? The only business he had was getting back into bed with her. She sighed with frustration.

'What is it?' he asked, feeling concerned

'I want you.' She moaned. '*Now.*' Reaching out her hand towards him, he got the message. It wasn't a request, it was a demand. Sequoia Lissen wanted hot, fast, wild, crazy sex, and she did not want to wait.

'Do you just?' Ruben looked at his watch, and growled. After last night, he never wanted to rush lovemaking again.

'I need to be there in half an hour.'

'That's plenty of time,' she smiled with her come-to-bed eyes.

Oh yes, she wanted him. Now! And he gave her everything he had, then and there. One thing was for certain, he would not be thinking straight when he sat in the boardroom in twenty-five minutes' time! *Oh Lord!* They exploded at the same time.

No hotel in the world, no matter how carefully crafted, offered this amount of luxury and opulence. No amount of money could buy this. Ruben kissed her tenderly. 'Hate to love you and leave you,' he said, dressing himself, and running his fingers through his hair.

'You can make it up to me later,' she said, unable to remove the smile from her face. She lay back in the sheets, luxuriating in the scent she was emitting: their combined scent, and sighed. Oh he made her feel good!

Sequoia admitted to herself that she felt good. Much better, in fact, than she had been. Stepping into the shower, she marvelled at the world of difference between her white, plastic-boxed shower which could barely fit a cat, and his shower, European style: it could fit a whole family, had two shower heads, and was contained in curved marble walls. Sequoia decided she could actually stay in there all day. It was the height of luxury, listening to the inbuilt stereo.

Revelling in the luxury, she sampled each of the scented shampoos and body washes, and used the loofah to brush her back.

The towels were somewhat different to the ones she had at home. His towels were suitable for a princess. And that was fine by Sequoia, for today she did indeed feel like royalty. Well-loved royalty!

Sequoia wandered into the living room, and Adagio came bounding up. Bending down to pick up the bundle of purr, she noticed Marion in the corner of the room dusting the piano.

'Good morning my dear,' she said warmly. 'Feeling better?'

'Quite a lot actually, thank you.'

'I've made some lunch if you like,' she said, pointing to the dining table. 'I've kept it simple. I know your appetite won't be back properly yet.'

'Do you have children, Marion?' Sequoia asked.

'Six!' she beamed. 'Six beautiful children.'

'Wow. I can't get my head around mothering one child. How did you do it?'

Marion laughed. 'One day at a time. And actually, raising one child is harder than raising six.'

Sequoia looked perplexed.

'When you have one child, you're the whole world to them. Once more children come along, there are other things to focus their attention. It makes a mother's life a bit easier,' Marion promised.

And Sequoia wondered, for the first time, what it might be like to have more than one child: to have a large family. But that would never happen. Not when she was leaving to go and become a single mother.

Sequoia sat down to her lunch: freshly baked rye bread, with slivers of creamy avocado, cucumber and basil leaves. 'Your friend Ali, from the café? She said it was your favourite.'

And just the mention of Ali's name brought tears to her eyes.

'I've really abandoned her down there. I can't imagine how she's coping,' Sequoia confided.

'Oh I wouldn't worry about that. Ruben's got it all in hand.'

A puzzled look crept across her face.

'He figured it would take three people to replace you, and moved three of the chefs from the hotel down there while you're here.'

'Really? He did that?'

'Oh yes, he's really thoughtful when people are suffering. One of the kindest men I know,' Marion said.

Sequoia felt like her mind was a see-saw. Yes, he was kind. Yes, he was one of the kindest men she knew, too...*except when he abandoned her in Tuscany!* And she could never forgive him for that!

Tonight she would ask him about his wife. In her mind, it had been a taboo subject, but now she was carrying his baby it was time for everything to come out in the open.

'I'm finishing in half an hour, so if there's anything you need, or anything you want from the shops, just let me know,' Marion said, putting away her cleaning bag.

It was about 2pm when a key turned in the front door. Sequoia's heart skipped a beat. Ruben was home!

All at once she felt like a schoolgirl, giddy and excitable. Only, when she looked up with joy, it was Hannah, the blonde bimbo. No, not a bimbo, apparently. Blonde brains.

'Oh, hello,' Hannah said, taken off guard. 'I wasn't expecting you here,' she mumbled, putting down her brief case.

I'll bet you didn't, Sequoia thought, her blood boiling. *No stress, the baby's listening.* She could hear the midwife's last words to her.

'Ruben about?'

'No, he's at a meeting. Was he expecting you?' Sequoia bristled.

'No, it was a surprise.' Their eyes met, each taking in the other. If this was high school, they'd have been scratching each other's eyes out by now.

'Make yourself comfortable then, if you're planning to wait for him,' Sequoia said, sitting on the sofa with Adagio.

And she couldn't help herself. Sequoia was feeling feisty. It was now or never. 'What were you and Ruben celebrating the day I came by and you were drinking champagne mid afternoon? It hardly looked like business!'

'Ruben didn't tell you?' was all Hannah had to say.

'You tell me.'

'We were celebrating a few things. A new venture he's just had approved. A hotel in each of the capital cities of Australia. They'd not only had planning permission go through without a hitch, but were already winning awards for ingenuity. I don't know why he wouldn't tell you something like that,' she snarled, 'he's so proud of it.'

Sequoia wanted to snarl back, but remembered the baby. *Everything* was centred on the baby.

'Why was he celebrating with you?' As much as it pained her to ask, she had to know the truth.

'I head his legal team. I've travelled with him to various countries where he has his line of hotels, and I will be overseeing the legal side of this new development. We also had some personal news he'd wanted to celebrate.'

Sequoia wanted her out, now. She didn't want this woman anywhere near Ruben. And then she caught herself. It's not like Ruben was hers, any more than she was his. Sequoia would be leaving soon, and then he could do what he wanted with the bimbo! The *brains*!

'I'm sure he'll take you along to all the hotels, if you're as serious as you think you are.'

Sequoia couldn't help but notice the satisfaction that Hannah was enjoying from watching her squirm. 'He'll need to oversee them at the commencement of development, at the very least. No, you wouldn't want to be away from him when he's in other cities, would you? Not with the way women fall at his feet all the time. It must be so disconcerting?'

That was the final straw.

'Shall I take a message for you then?' Sequoia asked, firmly asserting herself. 'I'll let Ruben know you came by.' With that, she picked up a book from the coffee table.

Ali visited at 4.30, and was beside herself with how attentive Ruben had been to the café. 'He comes by every day, checks the three chefs he brought in. Three chefs! There's hardly room in the kitchen to move.

Seriously, he must think we're running a hotel! And every morning, at the same time, there's a delivery from the Bay Market of fruits, vegetables and herbs. I don't even have to walk over and pick them up. The guy's a saint!'

Sequoia wasn't sure that she wanted to hear all that. Yes, she was relieved that she didn't have to give the café a thought while she got over the first hurdle of pregnancy, but did he actually have to take over?

'I heard Patrick's flown back to Belgium,' Ali said softly, watching Sequoia cringe. 'You're such a heartbreaker, Sequoia Lissen. Merciless! But really, a choice between puppy dog and rich saint? No choice, is there?'

'Ruben's a saint now, is he? Wasn't that long ago you were reminding me that he's a love rat. He can't be both!' she laughed.

They sat back on the sofa, their feet on the glass coffee table, enjoying the selection of fine dark chocolates that Sequoia had found in the pantry.

'This is the life, Sequoia; you've really landed on your feet.' Ali mused.

'I'm not staying here, Ali,' Sequoia informed her, a serious look clouding her face. 'Ruben's just looking after me for a bit. Then it's back to my life, my house, my...' but she couldn't say café, not when she was planning to leave Coles Bay.

Discord

Sequoia sulked as she paced the floorboards. It was 6pm, and hours after Ruben said he'd be home. To distract herself, she began playing the piano. At first, her fingers trembled as they touched the keys of such an exquisite instrument. Slowly she walked through the fear, and let herself come alive and relax. Each key, so perfectly crafted; and tuned at the right pitch. The sheen of the wood reflected her face. It was a *Faziola*, one of the most expensive and prized pianos in the world: not something you'd find in a person's home, but in a concert hall.

It was while she was playing and singing *Come Away With Me* that Ruben walked through the door.

'I'm so sorry I'm late,' he whispered, his hands on her shoulders. 'Don't stop. Keep playing.'

'Actually, I'm a bit tired. I think I'll go to bed,' she said, avoiding eye contact and aware that she was not behaving like the woman he'd been in bed with this morning, or indeed, last night.

'What the hell has happened?' he demanded. 'Sequoia?'

'Nothing, I'm just tired. I'll see you tomorrow.'

'No. Something's wrong, and you're not going to sleep until you tell me what it is. Come here,' he said, leading her to one of the sofas. 'Please sit.'

'Nothing's wrong. It's just time to stop playing happy families.' she said, fiddling with the hem of her tunic, something she did whenever she was nervous or insecure.

'You didn't feel like that this morning. What's going on?'

132

'Your friend Hannah came by. Let's just say it opened my eyes. Now, if you don't mind, I really do want to go to sleep.'

'If I don't mind? Of course I mind! What did she say?'

'It's what she didn't say Ruben. Clearly a woman who has the key to your house, and who can turn up uninvited, is more than the head of your legal team! Stop treating me as if I'm stupid. I'm not! Hannah told me you were both celebrating a personal matter, and she couldn't share it with me.'

'Not so fast,' he said, his hot breath coming down across her face.

When Ruben's mouth encircled hers, and his hands firmly against her back insisted that there was no intimacy between him and Hannah, Sequoia searched his eyes looking for answers.

'Nothing has happened between me and Hannah, and nothing ever will. I've never even looked sideways at the woman!' he protested.

'Do you really think I'm going to believe that? And one other question: where is your wife?'

And that last question floored him just as she intended.

'My *wife*? I haven't been married to her for some time. Do you really,' shaking his head in exasperation, 'think I'd have followed you to the other side of the world if I was still married?'

Sequoia wanted to believe him, but no longer knew what was real and true.

'Why does Hannah act as if you two are seeing each other, and I'm nothing more than a silly school girl with a one-way crush?'

'I don't know. She's just,' shaking his head, 'female

133

lawyers; they're not like normal women. I find they're hard, calculating. It's an occupational hazard. I can't explain her and frankly, Sequoia, I shouldn't need to. My word should be enough for you.'

Something shifted for Sequoia, and hardened her resolve to leave the bay as soon as she could. Ruben didn't attempt to make love to her that day; and in bed, they slept with their backs to each other. Despite all their history, and the years apart where she longed for him to be by her side, she'd never felt more alone in her life than in that moment.

Ruben arrived back home from a meeting several days later to find Sequoia had gone. In her place was a simple note: *Thanks for everything, Sequoia and Adagio.*

Ruben flinched. He'd never imagined her going back to her little wooden cabin. Sure, it was tastefully decorated, and homey, but he hoped she'd felt like that about his home. He'd done everything he could to ensure it had the feminine touch: large vases of flowers, lush tropical plants, throws over the sofa, magazines to read, an assortment of music, delicious food.

For years, he'd known that the only way to win her back was to give her something she couldn't say no to.

Over the next couple of weeks, the morning sickness eased to zero. When Sequoia returned to work, Ali was delirious. She'd been grateful for the Hazelwood chefs, and they were fabulous, but Sequoia's food was what the locals wanted to eat. Food made with love and passion.

Sequoia was going to have to break the news to Ali that she'd be selling *Treble Clef*, and that she could have first option of taking over the lease. Not today, though. Today she just wanted to make it through the morning. Ruben had phoned every day, and most days had come around to check on her. Last night she let him know, in no uncertain terms, that there was no future for them and that she was moving on. Ruben left, not saying a word. When he didn't fight for her, when he didn't protest, she realised that she'd made the right decision. Today was the hardest day of her life.

The Other Woman

It had been a long day in the café. Sequoia rubbed her achingly tired legs. In an hour, she'd be home and soaking in a tub of soothing bubbly water by candlelight. At bang on four o-clock, impatient to go home, she locked the front door and stood by it while staring at the beach. Ali was chattering away to her while replying to text messages on her phone. When there was no reply she asked 'What are you looking at?'

'There's someone on the beach I recognise, but I can't quite place her. She's not a local, but I feel like I've seen her before. Maybe an actress? I just can't jog my memory, and it's frustrating me.' Sequoia pointed towards the tall, dark Middle Eastern woman.

'Sweet Jesus!' Ali let out a whoop. 'I'll tell you who the hell it is!' Ali was spitting chips; her reaction startled Sequoia.

'You really don't know who it is?' Ali asked. 'Remember when you first told me about Ruben "the Love Rat"? Well, I googled him,' she flushed, feeling guilty. 'That woman on the beach? I'm almost certain she's his wife!'

Sequoia swayed, and reached for the nearest chair so she could sit down. 'You're right. I...oh God. How could I have been so stupid?' Sequoia wondered if she knew about the baby. Is that why she was here? To seek revenge? A cold shiver went up her spine.

'I better walk you home so you don't kill her,' Ali volunteered.

'No, I'm not going anywhere. I'll stay here for a while. I don't know what I was thinking.' Sequoia could hear the midwife's advice of keeping calm for the baby, but right now she wanted to scream. Why was Ruben here? Why did he have to do this to her?

Ali left, reluctantly, and Sequoia busied herself with planning the next month's menu. Committed to utilising local produce, and cooking to the seasons, this focus allowed her to settle herself. After half an hour of utter distraction, she was completely in the flow of creative variations on seasonal vegetables.

It was the gentle knock at the door which made her jump back to the present moment. Looking back over her shoulder, Sequoia turned to see who was there. Momentarily paralysed with fear, she saw that it was Ruben's wife standing there. Although she appeared timid, the woman's eyes beckoned Sequoia to let her in.

Slowly, Sequoia walked to the door and unlocked it. 'Can I help you?' she asked, scared to make eye contact.

'I'm hoping I can help you,' the lady offered.

'I know who you are, and I really don't see the point in us having any sort of discussion. My past is over. I have no interest in seeing Ruben Hazelwood, or indeed getting in the way of your marriage. Now, if you don't mind, I'm busy.' She reached to close the door, but the lady stopped her.

'Please. This is important.'

Sequoia let out a long sigh. 'Come in, then,' she said, raising her eyebrows in resignation.

Sequoia ushered her to a chair, and offered her a drink but she declined.

'My name was Madalina,' she offered quietly, 'but you will know me as Mihan Malek, the "mystery woman" who married Ruben.'

'I know who you are, but I don't know why you're here,' Sequoia flustered. What would Ruben make of his two lovers sitting together? She wondered if Ruben knew Mihan was here, in her café.

'I want to offer my deepest condolences for what you went through. It wasn't fair.'

'You're damn right it wasn't fair! I loved him!' and Sequoia was astounded by her outburst. Eight years of pent up anger came hurling out at this woman, when, in fact, she should have been yelling at Ruben. Even though she was aware that she was taking it out on the wrong person, in that moment she didn't care.

'I know you're angry, and you have every right to be. I don't deny you that, I would never dream of denying you that, but please, *please* hear me out.'

Sequoia was moved by her sincerity and gentleness, and tried to match it by regaining her composure.

'I am from Iran,' the lady said nervously. 'That is my homeland. I had been married to a bully. A violent man. He beat me every day, and raped me most days. Where I come from, a woman's voice is not heard.'

In a moment of shame, she bowed her head low as if she was to blame for his indulgent brutality.

'When he beat me so severely that I could hardly walk, I knew I had to escape. My life hung in the balance. By this point, he was so desensitised to how he treated me that he had no awareness of the full extent of his brutality or how cruel his demands were. But that was the last time he was ever going to touch me. I didn't get very far, just to an old shed on the outskirts of town. I was in such pain I lay there for a week trying to recover. I couldn't walk, and was starving. I hadn't had time to bring food, just water. My crying sounds caught the attention of a holidaymaker who was cycling past the old shed.' Mihan cried as she recalled this part of her story.

'His name was Maximus Millington.'

'Max? Max found you? Max Millington as in Ruben's best friend?' Sequoia asked, but she didn't need to frame it as a question. She knew exactly who he was for he'd accompanied Ruben and Sequoia to several events in London, and stayed with them for a while in Scotland.

'Max found me, and he took me back to his hotel and mended me. I was too scared to go to a doctor. I'd have only been sent back to my husband.'

'Then what happened?' Sequoia asked, on the verge of tears at the woman's plight.

'I stayed with Max for a few weeks, too afraid to go anywhere. In the meantime, we fell in love with each other. He was unlike any man I ever knew. Kind, caring, generous; he was a true gentleman.'

'Yes, he is a gentleman. That's for sure,' Sequoia agreed, recalling how kind he was to her after the British Press tore her to shreds.

'We left my home town, and settled in to a small village fifty miles away. I was in the market one morning with Max, when an acquaintance of my husband saw me. I was terrified for my life. You see, I was a married woman and my husband would know that Max and I were lovers. In my homeland, if a woman is unfaithful she is condemned to death by stoning.'

Sequoia reached out her hand, horrified at such a thought.

'I had no idea. But what's Ruben got to do with any of this?'

'Well, Max smuggled me out of Iran, brought me into Europe, and used his contacts, well, Ruben's contacts and money, to get me a new name—a new identity—and into England. But, I could only stay there

139

if I was married. I couldn't stay as a single woman. Ruben's influence didn't extend that far.'

'So why didn't you marry Max?' Sequoia was confused.

'He came to Iran when his marriage ended. He was on a healing journey. His wife was stalling the divorce, and marrying him just wasn't an option. We were racing against the clock. Racing time. My visa was soon to expire. If I had to return to my homeland, I would be discovered. I wouldn't be able to stay in hiding. I would have been killed.'

Sequoia could sense how important it was for her to tell this story and for her to be heard.

'Max begged Ruben to marry me. To protect me, and the life of our unborn child. I was pregnant.'

Sequoia's mind raced to her lovemaking with Ruben in Tuscany, and the horror on his face when he'd left her in the dead of night. It was starting to make sense. Except for one thing: why didn't he just *tell* her? Why didn't he explain it to her? Surely she'd have understood?

'Ruben felt powerless to refuse,' Mihan confided. 'He was always a bit of a humanitarian, according to Max, but he also owed him.'

'What do you mean, he "owed" him. Ruben has more money than any man I've ever met. I can't imagine him owing anyone anything. Ever,' Sequoia said, frustrated.

'When they were eighteen,' Mihan sighed, 'they were skiing in a resort in Switzerland with some of their friends. An avalanche fell down around them, and everyone got out of the way, except Ruben who had his legs pinned under a tree which come down.'

Sequoia grabbed her chest as if about to faint.

'What happened?' But she wasn't sure she really wanted to know. The thought of him being hurt, being in pain, suffering, was too much to take.

'Max wouldn't leave his side. He risked his own life, and they both nearly died. Ruben was close to death. He's never told you this story?' Mihan asked, shaking her head.

'No, never.'

Frustrated that he'd keep such a momentous, life-changing event to himself, she wondered why didn't he open up to her about such things.

'Max looked Ruben in the eyes and said "I've known you all of our lives. I'm not leaving you. You can pay me back one day," and Ruben laughed, but even in jest, and even while drifting in and out of consciousness, he held onto those words. Those words got him through. He said "I promise, Max, if there's anything you ever need, I'll be there without hesitation". He knew there was no amount of money in the world that could repay Max. It would need to be a grand gesture. A life for a life.'

Sequoia was crying, and felt Mihan put her arms around her, before she continued speaking.

'I promise you with all of my heart that everything about my relationship with Ruben is platonic. Nothing, but gratitude. I can never go home. I can never contact my family again. I have to keep my new identity a secret. I travel on a forged passport terrified for my life whenever I enter a new country. I live in fear, but here, in Australia, I feel safe. Sequoia, sometimes money can buy things. Ruben tells me you have a lot of disdain for his wealth, his money, his lifestyle, but I would be dead right now if it weren't for his generosity, kindness and compassion. Look over there,' Mihan said, pointing to

141

a man and a young boy on the beach, kicking a ball. 'That's Max, and our son Alexander.'

'Ruben's middle name?' Sequoia asked.

'Yes.'

Sequoia smiled, and recognised Max. She'd enjoyed his humour, and mischievous smile and knew he was a good man. She remembered, too, that he'd been devastated by the end of his marriage, and Ruben had spent a lot of time trying to keep him propped up; caring greatly about his mental wellbeing.

'We've moved to Coles Bay for a new life. Sequoia, I hope you and I can be friends. I know it is a lot to ask. For eight years, I've been the other woman. You have every right to hate me, but please believe me when I say that my love for Ruben, and I *do* love him, of that you can be sure, is based on gratitude.'

'Why didn't he tell me?' Sequoia asked. 'I would have understood. I might have been young, inexperienced, but I really would have understood. I would have cried, I would have been upset, but I really would have let him marry you.'

In an intimate, bonding gesture of sisterhood, Mihan wiped the tears from Sequoia's cheeks.

'He never stopped talking about you. I feel like I know everything about you. It's like you're my sister. I could write a book about you.' She smiled, touched her arm affectionately and then said, 'Our marriage was annulled when I'd been in England long enough to gain residency. Ruben was patient, but he was so miserable. Despite his own pain, and Sequoia, you have to know he was emotionally conflicted, in utter turmoil, yet he was a tower of support for me. Always strong. Unhappy, but strong,' she said. 'Perhaps I will have a drink now.'

142

Sequoia walked behind the counter, and reached into the fridge for homemade lemonade.

After a few sips, Mihan continued. 'Ruben couldn't understand why you didn't phone him, or reply to his letter. And when you disappeared he swore not to rest until he'd found you. At one time, he had seven private investigators trying to find you. He sacked four of them when they said you'd disappeared without a trace. You were determined to start a new life, weren't you?'

'Yes, I was. He's never told me any of this. I was completely in the dark.'

'But even though he knew that you were moving on with your life, he couldn't be sure. He was so worried, so beside himself with fear that you'd taken your life. In the meantime, he started designing buildings; first-class hotels, each one designed with you in mind. He sued several British tabloids on your behalf for what they wrote about you, and then donated the money to an orphanage near your village in France.'

'Ruben did that? For me?'

'Yes. He travelled to different countries, and imagined you living there. It wasn't long until he gave up on the private investigators, and started asking himself what would make you sing. What would make you think "this is home". He knew for certain that you'd be working with food, and he said that the word "sunshine" kept coming into his mind. And how your smile was like sunshine.'

Mihan flushed red, and added 'He said how you described lovemaking as like liquid sunshine, and he knew that you would be somewhere that felt like that.'

'Did he just?' and Sequoia couldn't help let out a little embarrassed laugh.

'It was after a couple of bottles of wine,' Mihan

admitted. 'He wouldn't have shared something so personal if he wasn't drunk. A chance conversation with an Aussie tourist, while he was in Argentina overseeing the building of the Sequoia Royale ...'

'The *what*?' she laughed out loud.

'That's what most of his hotels are called,' Mihan smiled. 'I'm surprised you've never heard of them. They're quite the talk in the hotel industry. Anyway, the tourist said he'd just come from Coles Bay in Tasmania which had 300 days of sunshine a year. Ruben said something inside him clicked, like a light turning on, and he knew...just *knew*.'

'But lots of places have sunshine,' Sequoia said.

'Yes, but he remembered the first time he heard you speak, and he was trying to pick up your accent, and he thought he'd heard vague echoes of Australian beneath the hybrid French, American and English accent. He was on the first plane to Melbourne, straight into Hobart, and drove to Coles Bay.'

'When was that?' Sequoia asked.

'Three years ago.'

'Three years ago? Why did he wait so long to make his presence known?'

'He saw you working in a fish and chip shop, and felt your talents were wasted, but he was stunned by how happy you looked. He didn't want to ruin that.' Mihan smiled. 'He sought planning permission from the council to build Hazelwood Hotel. When *Treble Clef* opened, he phoned us in England. Oh Sequoia, he sounded like the happiest man in the whole world. Ruben was so proud of you. He said he knew you'd succeed. And most importantly, he knew he could never have bought that for you.' Mihan reached for Sequoia's hands.

144

'He said watching you taught him the true value of success. Give him a chance. He knew you were the right one, the only one, for him from the day he met you in the bakery. I know he's a man who can click his fingers and have any woman he wants, and how they hang off his every word. But he's been faithful to you and your memory. He's not even indulged in physical release. Not once. There aren't many men on the planet who'd do that. Ruben thought he knew what he was looking for in life, but he didn't know at all until he met you.'

'This is too much information to take in. I need to be alone now. To process this. I like you Mihan, I really do. I'd like to believe you, that all this is true. I just wish he'd told me. Wish he'd *protected* me from the world.'

'He'd have done anything to protect you.'

Sequoia cut her off. 'But he didn't! He didn't do anything!'

'And he will live the rest of his life regretting that. Eight years without you, now that's a huge regret,' Mihan said solemnly. 'Don't waste any more time apart.'

Mihan started to walk away, and then turned around.

'Sequoia, if there's anything I learned from his endless monologues about you, it is this: if there was anyone who could go through an experience like you did, and survive, it was you. It takes enormous character and intelligence to not only protect yourself in the way you did, but to then go on and live a life like this?' she said, her hands spread to indicate the beautiful café around them, 'A life where you are positively thriving. *You* did that. I didn't. Ruben and Max saved me. I didn't have the strength that you did.' Mihan wept.

145

'Mihan,' Sequoia said gently, 'I couldn't have survived what *you* went through with your husband. My experience was a piece of cake in comparison. Don't underestimate your own strength. And the strength that it took for you to come here today. That can't have been easy. I'm sorry for how I spoke to you.'

Mihan's head hung low, and then she looked thoughtfully at Sequoia unsure of how much more she should share.

'I've never heard a grown man cry like Ruben did for the months after he was apart from you. I often wondered if my peace, and my baby's life, was worth that amount of pain. It wasn't fair. Not fair for any of us. I hated myself for it. Ruben became a hermit, and spent a lot of time in Scotland completely isolating himself. Max and I moved in with him, and he made sure we were really well looked after. I had the best independent midwives hired from London, maids, a cook, well, everything you could only dream of when you're a new mother. The privileged life he leads was shared with me, and was my blessing and my balm. He worked on his designs night and day, and was winning awards before his buildings were even constructed. Some have said his architecture is nothing short of genius.'

'He hasn't told me that,' Sequoia said.

'You haven't given him a chance!' Mihan said, rather indignantly.

'That's true. I haven't,' and she felt herself cringe inside.

'Go and talk to him,' Mihan encouraged.

'I can't. I've spent eight years trying to exorcise him from me. I've tried to hate him. But this? I'm not worthy of such a kind and compassionate man!'

'Go to him,' Mihan said gently. 'He needs you. *He needs you.*'

'I was horrible to him at the ball. I could see it in his eyes, but I really wanted to hurt him. I wanted him to feel some of my pain, even an inch of it. And I've said some rather unkind things since then, too.'

'Ruben has no idea that you don't know what really happened. He sent you a signed-for courier-delivered letter, explaining everything, and asking you to wait. Ruben thinks you know everything, and that you simply couldn't be bothered to wait.'

'I got the letter,' Sequoia sighed. 'I signed for it. That part is true. But I threw it out. I never gave a thought to what was inside it. I was so humiliated, so hurt...'

'He'll forgive your harsh words. This is the man who'd buy the whole world for you!'

Sequoia cried. 'I don't want him to buy the whole world for me,' she yelled out in frustration. 'I want to *be* his whole world!'

'Then get out of that chair and tell him!'

Beneath the Scar

Sequoia spied Jack on the pavement, outside *Bay Books*, as she let Mihan out the front door of the café and waved her goodbye. They hadn't spoken properly since the ball, and then when his mother died, he'd retreated. Now was as good a time as any to apologise, but she really wanted to see Ruben first. Their eyes caught, and he smiled meekly. *Now or never*, Sequoia thought to herself.

'I wondered if you'd been avoiding me,' Jack said dejectedly.

'No Jack, I just didn't want either of us to be uncomfortable. Fancy a walk on the waterfront?' she asked, and was astonished at how such a simple question could light up his whole face.

They crossed the road together, then Sequoia slipped off her shoes and let the sand cushion her toes and heels. It had been a long day, and she was still reeling from Mihan's story.

'I'm sorry I didn't tell you about Ruben. The truth is, I wasn't sure it was him who owned the hotel. Not straight away, at least. We knew each other eight years ago.'

'Yet your body language indicates it was just yesterday that you'd been together.' He interjected, wanting to let her know he was onto them.

'I loved him, Jack! And... he loved me,' she said hoping he'd understand the significance of their past. Maybe it would help him find a way through her rejection of him.

Jack took her hand in his. 'Let me give you an uncomplicated life. No drama. No pain. I promise to be

148

kind,' he said, wiping a tear from her eye. 'Why would any man be stupid enough to let a woman like you go? It doesn't make sense!' Jack kicked the sand in anger.

'He had his reasons,' she said gently. Mihan's story was not hers to tell; just hers to protect. And that, she would. Right now, she regretted stopping to talk to Jack and wished she'd gone straight home. More than anything, she needed time to think about Mihan, Max, Alexander, and Ruben. *Especially* Ruben! The consequences of not reading his letter eight years ago weighed heavily on her mind.

'Don't make excuses for him! Damn it! If a man wants you Sequoia, nothing, nothing can keep him away.' From the way he looked at her, she sensed he was hoping to break through the wall she was erecting. It was obvious Jack wanted her so badly. 'If a man doesn't want you, nothing can make him stay with you.'

'I know that Jack. I know.'

Thinking of her baby, she tried to calm down and settle her heartbeat.

'So, are you lovers again? Did you sleep with him after the ball?' he asked, gripping her wrist tightly, making her pulse flee in fright.

Relax, baby. Relax.

'Lovers, friends? What are you?' He snapped. 'I need to know where I stand!'

Sequoia had never seen this side of Jack before: like a tom cat marking his territory; and she felt more than a bit frightened.

'Jack, I really think you're a lovely man. That is true. And if Ruben hadn't turned up, then who knows? But my heart is elsewhere. I can't lie about that.'

'You can't change a man, Sequoia. Don't let Hazelwood think he's more important than you are just because he's richer than ten banks put together. He's not God! He's just a man. Just a man! He's no better than any of the rest of us. Why are you so blind to that?'

'Jack...' but she couldn't say anything else, because he forced her into his arms, and wrenched her tightly into his. Terrified, a scream escaped her lips as she tried pulling away. A passerby stopped and asked if she was alright.

'Jack, let me go,' she said, staggering backwards in the sand.

Jack came back to reality with a jolt. 'So you'll choose him over me, then?'

'I'm so sorry Jack. I'm so sorry.' With trembling lips, she walked away, and headed home, sick to the stomach, her head spinning. What the hell just happened?

As Sequoia reached the roadside, she saw a black BMW pull away, its screeching tyres leaving black marks on the bitumen. *Ruben!* Had he just seen Jack kissing her? Why was he leaving? Surely he didn't think there was anything going on? Didn't he see how she pushed him away? Didn't he see how the stranger came up to them? Didn't he see her run off? Her heart was falling apart. Just when things seemed hopeful! Just when she'd finally understood. She tried phoning him, but the answering machine kept clicking in. Of course she should just drive to his home. It was that simple, really. But she wasn't ready. There was too much to digest, and to reconsider her part in their broken love story. If only she'd read his letter that morning in France, instead of throwing it, unopened, straight into the wood-fired oven, things might have turned out differently.

Ruben had always assumed she *knew* why he married Mihan. And when she disappeared, he assumed that she wasn't prepared to wait. She had to tell him, but when? How?

After an hour of padding barefoot nervously, back and forth on her wooden floors, Sequoia finally sat down to check emails. Within minutes of perching herself in front of the laptop, she was googling locations on the mainland; searching for places that might prove to be a good home for her and the baby, when something—she didn't know what—made her type *Ruben Hazelwood* into the search engine. Why she'd never done this before, was beyond her. Even Ali, the techno-phobe, had managed to google-search Ruben the Love Rat!

There were pages and pages and pages of Hazelwood entries, media stories, including the ones about Sequoia being his brief fling, which she studiously avoided; his family history, property ownership, listings in Debretts, and many pages later even the story about the skiing accident. It was the heading: *Hazelwood Tragedy Leaves Son As Only Heir* that caught her eye. With hands shaking unsteadily, she clicked the laptop mouse. Surely it must be a different family?

It was a newspaper piece in *The London Times*, from more thirty years ago. A shiver forced itself up her spine before she dared herself to read.

William James Benjamin Hazelwood, aged two, was killed yesterday in a drowning accident at the family home in London.

Police say that his older brother's bike was lying on the side of the pool. The toddler tripped over it, and he hit his head on the side before falling in and drowning. The death has shocked the City. It leaves Fenton Hazelwood with just one heir: five-year-old Ruben Alexander Hazelwood.

Tears slipped from her eyes and her sobbing soon had Adagio climbing onto her lap. In all the conversations that she'd shared with Ruben, he'd never once mentioned this story. The only thing he'd ever said was that he was an only child, and that was why he liked to spend time on his own.

Did he blame himself for his brother's death? Is that why everything had to be "just so"; everything kept immaculate and in order? Oh how her heart ached. And then, she felt her baby kick. *Their baby.* She wanted Ruben to feel it too, to tell him that finally she understood why he was so controlling. But she'd made her decision. Just as he had his reasons for never sharing this childhood-changing, life-changing story, so too did she had her reasons for moving on. Sequoia may have forgiven him, but he'd chosen to let her walk away. That one decision sealed their fate.

But still, she kept reading like a woman obsessed, and clicking on links to media stories. It was as if someone had punched her pregnant belly three times in quick succession.

Glendaline Hazelwood
sectioned under the mental health act

What?

The story before her eyes was like something from a movie. It surely couldn't have happened? Unable to deal with the grief of her son's death, Mrs Hazelwood had attempted suicide. For her own safety, her husband had her placed into a mental institution. He'd hoped it would escape media attention.

Sequoia closed her eyes, imagining Ruben as a young boy. Losing his brother in such an awful way, and then his mother like that. Through her tears, she thought of how when Ruben introduced her to his parents, she mistook the haunted look in his mother's eyes to mean she disliked, perhaps even distrusted, Sequoia. But then she was confused when Mrs Hazelwood took her aside in the ladies' room, one night after a charity fundraiser, and hugged her tight. She simply said, 'Look after my Ruben.' It all made sense now. Everything was making sense.

Sequoia needed to go for a walk. She desperately needed fresh air. Just as she was about to log off, she noticed another entry and couldn't ignore it.

```
Hazelwood Nanny Killed
   in Tragic Car Accident
```

No! No! No! Surely not another tragedy?

```
Ellie Anderson, nanny to the
young Hazelwood heir, was killed
today in a tragic accident, when
the car she was driving skidded
on black ice. Nine-year-old
Ruben Hazelwood was unharmed.
Ellie was well-known in Chelsea
as a dedicated concert pianist,
and retired from professional
playing to take up the position
in the family home in the
absence of Mrs Hazelwood.
```

Hadn't Ruben valued Sequoia enough to share these events, no matter how painful they were? Sick to her stomach, Sequoia recoiled as she remembered the harsh words she threw at him about how he had no insights into grief. If only she could take back her barbed words, and replace them with hugs.

Sequoia turned off the laptop, and had a long, long shower. Right now she was standing at the crossroads of life, and in that moment realised there wasn't actually a choice to make. Ruben had let her go, and now it was time for her to do so. Time for her to leave Coles Bay. Tomorrow, she'd put things in motion. But for now, all she wanted to do was close her eyes and rid herself of the painful images in her head. And she wondered how Ruben had lived with this for all these years.

Love Child

Sequoia was sitting on her bottom as she weeded her front garden. Ruben, no doubt, would have thought she looked cute if he'd seen her dressed in the hot-pink floral dungarees. With dirt on her nose, and fingers in the soil, she felt great. No sickness, just a big blooming belly. As long as she didn't think of Ruben, then everything in her life would be fine. *Just fine*, she kept telling herself. Except for the fact that she was leaving Coles Bay next week; leaving the home she'd created, and the place she loved.

Ruben hadn't fought her decision to put the café into Ali's name, and everything had been handled by solicitors so they didn't have to see each other. The landlord of her house was happy for her to pass the tenancy to someone else. Everything was going smoothly. The only job she had left to do was to weed and tidy up the front garden. The sunshine on her skin gave her hope. As she held her face up to the summer sunshine, basking in the rays, she felt warmth, joy and pleasure. Sequoia promised herself that this new beginning was in everyone's best interests. Jack's words continued to haunt her: 'If a man wants a woman, nothing but nothing will stop him being with her. And if he doesn't want a woman, nothing can make him stay.' *Not even a baby.* Deep in thought, she barely heard the motor just a few metres away.

A rental car pulled up in front of her. Within seconds, a towering man with sandy-coloured hair, in his early fifties, got out and headed towards her. Deliciously tanned, with crow's-feet embedded at the corners of his eyes, his face spoke of someone who lived a happy and easy life. Everything about him reminded her of sunshine: warmth, light, calm. His handsome features and relaxed face exuded friendliness. There was something vaguely familiar about him, but she couldn't place him. Sequoia rummaged through memories; old, *old* memories. It was if he was there, but not quite there. It was as if she knew him intimately, but she was one hundred percent certain that she'd never actually seen him before.

'Sequoia? Sequoia *Lissen*?' he asked. His American accent was warm and friendly.

'Yes, that's me. May I help you?' she asked, finally standing up.

'My name is Scott. Scott Mitchell. We've never met. Forgive the intrusion. I don't know how to say this. I'm your father.'

All at once, she sank down to the ground, and he reached down to support her.

'Are you okay?' he asked. 'I'm sorry, I realise it's a bit of a shock. There was no easy way to say it, and believe me I rehearsed that line a lot!'

Never, never in her wildest dreams did she imagine such a scenario. Oh, yes, she'd imagined it. A million times over. What little girl wouldn't want to meet her daddy? But, she knew it was an impossibility!

'How?' as she struggled to find the words she asked 'Are you sure? You better come inside.'

Before they made it to the front door, Sequoia was sobbing uncontrollably.

'I'm sorry, pregnancy hormones' she said, pointing to her belly. And then she saw his eyes were filled with tears.

'What's my excuse then?' he laughed through the tears.

'I always wanted to have a daughter,' he confided. 'If only I'd known. You're so beautiful, and a spitting image of your mother. It's shocking how alike you are. I nearly had a heart attack when I saw you on the lawn weeding. It was like stepping back 28 years!'

'But, mother said you didn't know each other's surnames. How did you find me? How did you know about me?'

'Ruben Hazelwood.'

'Ruben?' she asked, and her voice croaked as if it was a toad being forced out backwards by its hind legs. 'No. Impossible. Ruben would have no more way of finding out who you were than anyone else.'

Sequoia rubbed her eyes. This was a game changer. Her baby, *their* baby, was going to have a grandparent from her side of the family! The joy mingled with shock was overwhelming.

'Hasn't he told you?' Scott asked, a little dumbfounded. 'I met up with him a few weeks ago. It was just after the feature article that was syndicated across America? Ruben flew to the US and we spent a couple of weeks together.'

'What feature article?' she asked nervously.

'Just wait a minute,' he said, and headed out to his car.

Sequoia noted that he might have been middle aged, but she could sure tell why her mother had been so besotted with him, and why she'd done something as irresponsible as have unprotected sex with a stranger.

Scott jogged down the garden path, his long body so typical of a Californian body surfer, then returned with a couple of magazines and the New York Times and Los Angeles Times newspapers.

Just reading those words had Sequoia crying again. Scott held her in his arms and whispered 'Just let it all out.'

The articles featured her mother's brief affair with Scott, and Ruben's quest to build a *Sequoia Royale* deluxe five-star hotel in all the major cities of the world; a mission that he'd continue until Sequoia's father was found. Each hotel had their love story on a sheet of paper, inside a gold frame, on the bedside table of every room. The articles included a photo of Sequoia and one of her late mother, the international hotels, and Ruben's contact details.

'It wasn't the article that caught my eye, and not even the name of the Sequoia National Park. I camped at a lot of parks that Summer! It was your photo. It stopped me dead in my tracks.' Scott recalled that moment, sitting on his patio in the morning Californian sunshine, sipping a mango smoothie. Having just returned from a jog on the beach, he was savouring the sweet drink while he read the paper. Suddenly, the glass fell from his hand and smashed on the tiles. Never in his wildest dreams did he guess that Katya had had his child.

Scott looked at Sequoia, tears still falling down her face.

'Come here,' he said, and wrapped his arms around her again. 'Let me hold my daughter,' and with that, she fell into his arms and cried, and cried, and cried. Sequoia imagined her mother there, her arms embracing them, and allowed this vision of love to feed her baby.

When she settled down, some time later, he said, 'I realise any man could come forward and say they were your dad because of the handsome reward offered, but just so you know: Ruben's already had me go through various DNA tests. Only one was necessary, but he wanted to make triple certain. I was happy to let him do those, and it's fair enough. But I knew as soon as I saw your photo. And I didn't need any reward money. You're the greatest reward of all.'

Sequoia spoke softly now, scared of the words coming out of her mouth: 'I can't believe Ruben did that for me. I can't believe he never told me.'

'From what I've seen, that man would do anything for you, anything at all. There's a depth of love there I've never seen in a human being.'

For a moment, she wondered how Ruben could have matched their DNA, and then assumed he probably bribed the midwife for blood results or hair or something. Deceptive, she thought, but effective.

Sequoia listened to her father all afternoon, taking in his Californian accent, and hearing about his life as the manager of a vineyard in Napa Valley. The Summer he'd met her mother, he'd been on an extended holiday. A year of freedom and recklessness; before taking over the vineyard, which had been in his family for a hundred years.

Sequoia brewed a pot of tea. Chamomile, to calm the nerves, and a coffee for her father. Adagio had found her way onto Scott's lap. The irony, Sequoia thought. Tomorrow, Adagio would be moving in with Ali.

'Mum and I lived in the US for the first five years of my life, travelling around California. We did a lot of camping. She was searching for you, you know. Not that she had much to go on!'

Scott smiled. 'No, not much at all. It's a miracle that we're sitting here today. Did she go back to France because she gave up?'

'No, not at all. Her father, my grandfather, was dying, and she felt it only fair to take over the family boulangerie.' Sequoia looked to the floor. 'No, she never gave up at all. Mum always dreamed that you'd walk through her front door. You need to know that, even though you weren't in my life, you were *always* there: larger than life. You were like God to me! There, but not there, if you know what I mean? I had so many secret conversations with you!' she laughed out loud, 'and when I saw you get out of the car today, I recognised you instantly without knowing why. Mum described you in so much detail; well, of course I'd recognise you.'

And then a thought occurred to her.

'Now that we've found each other, I can't bear the idea of us living across the world from each other. How would you feel if I moved to the US, and then you could see more of me and' she said, patting her belly 'your grandchild? I still have a US passport!'

When Scott's face visibly shifted, but not in the direction she'd hoped, Sequoia was taken aback. Although they'd only just met, she thought he'd be thrilled.

'That's not going to be possible. I'm sorry Sequoia. I'm moving. I'm starting a new job managing, um…I'm moving to Coles Bay, and I've just bought that huge vineyard overlooking Freycinet National Park. Ruben hasn't told you any of this?' he asked, disbelievingly. 'Hasn't told you a single thing?'

Breathe. Just breathe.

'Not a word…'

Damn it!

How was she supposed to leave Coles Bay now? And her house? Her café? Damn you Ruben Hazelwood. But she couldn't damn him, could she? Not now. Not with all this. Not when he'd given her yet another great gift. A child *and* her father.

'But what about your family vineyard? What will happen to that?' she asked, still not comprehending the new choices ahead of her.

'I have five younger brothers and two sisters. A few of them are taking over. That way it can still stay in the family.'

The smile on her face was contagious, and Scott's face lit up too.

'I have aunties and uncles?' she said, hand on her chest to contain her fluttering heart; tears trickling.

'Oh honey,' he said, 'you have aunties, uncles, twenty five cute and crazy cousins, and two healthy and active grandparents, all of whom are just so darn excited to meet you!'

'They know about me?' she asked in disbelief and wiped her tears.

'Did you really think I was going to be able to keep this news to myself?'

Once again, she sat back down, her breathing unsteady, and her mind racing.

'Do you have a wife?' she asked tentatively. 'Other children?'

'No.'

She wasn't sure how to read his answer.

'Your mother and I might have only been together for four days, Sequoia, but we lived a whole lifetime in those days and nights.'

'That's what mum said. "A whole lifetime!" They were her exact words.'

Scott smiled. 'It's true; we didn't know each other's surname. It seemed irrelevant, but on the fifth morning I intended to let her know where I lived, and how we could keep in touch when she'd finished her around-the-world-in-eighty-days trip of a lifetime. I returned from doing my laundry at the campsite only to find that the bus had come in a few minutes early, and I missed her.'

Sequoia was visibly shaken. 'It could have all been so different?'

'It could have, but it wasn't. I was so sorry to hear that she'd passed away, and from what Ruben said, it sounded like a slow and painful death.' Scott held her hand.

'It was,' she whimpered, nodding. 'It was.'

She looked up at him, 'Scott...'

'Dad. Please call me Dad. If you want to, that is. I've waited long enough to hear that.'

Laughter, mixed with crying, she asked 'Dad, why didn't you marry anyone else?'

'Why? Your mother ruined me for any other woman! I've dated, and cared for women, but marriage? No. No-one was ever going to compete with her memory. She was so incredible. Passionate. Strong. Feisty. In fact, Ruben tells me that sounds just like you,' he chuckled.

'Yes, I think he has called me those words once or twice.'

'And your mum? She never married?'

'She said you ruined her for any other man,' Sequoia smiled. 'Mum said there wasn't a man alive who could ever take her the way you did,' and she blushed. 'She didn't tell me *that* bit until I was eighteen!'

162

They held hands, and kept offering each other tissues. When Sequoia stepped into the garden that day to remove a few weeds, she had no idea what that would really mean. The weeds of her life were being plucked out, one by one, and all that was left were beautiful flowers. Now she had to gather them all together and arrange them carefully in the same vase.

Sequoia Royale

'I need a favour,' Sequoia asked Marion as she stood on the front steps of Ruben's mountain-side home. 'Can you let me in?'

'Ruben's not in dear. He'll be back in half an hour.'

'That's perfect. Can you let me in, and can you finish early? Please. This is important.'

'Yes, dear.' Marion had been told several times before by Ruben that in his home, Sequoia was to be treated like a princess, and nothing less. 'He hasn't been the same since you moved out. Crotchety, knit-picking, irritable. Please tell me you're here to stay? I want the old Ruben back.'

'I sure hope so,' she sighed, and spontaneously reached over to hug Marion. In that moment she realised that the kind woman had been a subtle mother figure to her when she'd convalesced here. Always hovering, bringing water, hot chocolate, blankets, dropping off books and magazines about parenting; and always ready for a gentle chat. Marion picked up her cleaning gear, and bid her farewell.

Sequoia stood in the heart of Ruben's immaculate living room, with its views over the bay. Home. Unless she was with Ruben, she'd never be settled. And nor would her baby. Their baby.

Her fingers glided along the top of the grand piano. *Tonight I will play for you*, she whispered over the top of it. *I will always play for you.*

When Ruben walked through the front door a little while later, Sequoia was playing the piano, singing the Eva Cassidy song *I Know You By Heart*.

'Why are you here?' his voice croaked.

Sequoia could see that he didn't trust himself not to cry and knew that the rest of his life was tied up in this moment. Every word had to be right. Nothing out of tone, nothing accusatory. For him, she had to get everything 'just so'. Finally, she understood that his life was always held on the balance of things being in the perfect order. There was no room for error.

'My father, Scott Mitchell, I believe you know him?' she asked, raising her eyebrows.

'Yes. I do. And a fine man he is. Not that I would have expected anything less would have gone into your DNA.'

'Come here, Sequoia,' he said calmly, with more than a hint of weariness, though she could see he was riddled with nerves. 'You're too far away.'

And within seconds, she was off the piano stool and in his arms.

'I can't believe what you did to find him,' she cried. 'I don't know if I will ever fully comprehend the magnitude of your kindness and determination and the extraordinary lengths you went to.'

'Love. It was only ever about *love*, Sequoia. I'd give you the Moon, if I could. Don't you know that by now? What else can I do to prove that you're the only person I ever want to be with? I'm consumed by you in every waking moment.'

'I don't want the Moon or the Sun or the stars in the sky,' she cried. 'Ruben, I only want *you*.'

Ruben kissed her, softly at first, then ravenously. He was hungry. Every kiss had to spell out one thing: this was it. No more cat and mouse, no more running away. This was them. Real. Now. Honest.

'I never read your letter,' she sobbed; her tear-soaked face looked up at him. 'I threw it out. I've spent eight years trying to hate you, and being unable to comprehend how the man I loved so much could break me into a million pieces.'

'You didn't know?' he asked incredulously, holding her close, his breathing rapid. 'You really thought I married someone else because I *wanted* to? You believed that of me?' He let go of her for a moment, and sat down. 'Would it have made any difference? The letter? Would you have waited? Would you have understood?'

'Ruben, I never stopped waiting for you. Never. I just needed to lick my wounds. I saw the engagement ring in Tuscany and I left there so darn happy! And then, not long after I saw you were married to someone else and your love story splashed on the front of the newspapers. What else could I do but run away?'

Ruben drew her close to him. Finally, they were together. Nothing was going to be in their way.

'God I've missed you,' he said, breathing in the scent of her. 'Not a single day goes by where I haven't had a thought of you. I never want to spend another night away from you.'

'You were so good to Mihan. It breaks my heart to think of what she went through; her and Max. And you. What *you* went through. That breaks my heart.'

'Just you remember,' he said, scooping her off the floor and carrying her to their bedroom, 'If I could do all that for a woman who was nothing more than a complete stranger, then what do you think I'll do for a woman I love with all my being?'

'I couldn't possibly imagine. You might have to show me,' she giggled, and she let him carry her to their bed. And slowly, ever so slowly, he began to show her just how very much he loved her.

Sleep wouldn't reach out to them tonight. It was a defining day, and was not going to be wasted on something as numbing as slumber. They lay in each other's arms, whispering, laughing, and loving.

'Honey, tell me about William and Ellie.'

Darkness shadowed Ruben's face, and for a moment, just a moment, Sequoia thought he was going to get angry, but then she realised it was a look of relief. The secret vault had been opened, and she was giving him permission to share. So, Ruben let her in to his dark world.

For a while, he remained quiet, as if trying to find words from a time without words; a time when *everything* was about feelings: a time where he was encouraged to lock every last tear away.

'Ruben, I want to know everything about you. And,' she hesitated, 'I want to hear it from you. Not secondhand through Mihan and Max, and most certainly not through Google. Talk to me, when you're ready. I'm here. I've always been here.'

Ruben sighed deeply, and buried his head against her soft skin. Resurfacing, he said, 'William and I were playing happily. I was riding my three-wheeler, and he was playing with a toy truck. Mum had just gone inside to answer a phone call. She told me to watch William, and that she'd be back in a minute. I got off my bike to go and play with him, and…' his voice croaked.

'It's okay, honey. It's okay to cry.'

'My father always told me it wasn't okay to cry. I was a Hazelwood, and Hazelwood men don't cry. They never have, he said. And I couldn't possibly break family tradition!'

Sequoia wanted to scream. What a stupid, stupid thing to say to a child. Didn't they have any idea of the untold damage that does to a boy? And how that haunts him for the rest of his life?

'Will and I started chasing each other, laughing, and having fun. But then...' he stumbled on his words, 'then he ran back towards my bike and tumbled over it.' A shudder ran through Ruben. It was an image he'd run through his head millions of times, but it still felt like a sword through his heart. Sequoia saw him wince as he relived the fateful scene.

'I heard his head crack, and he fell over into the pool. I called Mum, but she didn't hear me. I screamed. I couldn't swim. I didn't know what to do. I ran inside to get her, pulling her by the skirt of her dress. By the time she'd got out there, and then came back in to call an ambulance, it was too late. My mother had no first-aid skills, and was in such a state of panic that she didn't do anything obvious, like pull him out of the pool and clear his throat or mouth. If only she'd pulled him out. There might have been a chance.'

'Why do you feel like William's death was your fault?'

Ruben looked up at her.

'I was supposed to be looking after him. It was only for a minute. That's what Mum said. And, and if my bike had been put upright near a railing like my father had taught me to do on the day he bought it, instead of by the pool, he wouldn't have tripped and fell. Of course it's my fault!'

'Ruben, look at me,' she said firmly. 'It was not your fault. It never was. William's death was one of those sad and tragic life events. But it was *never* your fault.'

Sequoia cradled him in her arms, furious that Ruben had carried that level of guilt for almost his whole life. 'You were just a little boy. Little! You shouldn't have been responsible for babysitting him, even for a minute; the bike was part of his destiny. You weren't careless, Ruben.'

A long, deep breath of relief surged from his lungs.

'I said things to you, about you not understanding grief, and I'm so sorry. You told me that day not to say anything that I might come to regret. Oh Ruben. I'm so sorry. Can you forgive me? I wish I could take those words back,' she whispered, a tear trickling from her eye.

'You have the right to regret, we all do. It's an important part of life. There's nothing for me to forgive,' and he kissed her gently on her shoulder.

'Shall I get us a cup of tea?' she asked kindly.

'Yeah, that would be great.'

Ruben followed her into the kitchen, his arms never far from her naked waist.

'And Ellie. Ellie Sanderson. Tell me about her.'

'You probably know from your friend Mr Google that my mother was sectioned after trying to poison herself?'

'Yes, honey. I do.'

If only she could wind back the clock of his life so she could make everything 'just so', and give him a childhood of love, peace, affection and warmth.

'I already knew Ellie. My mother and her were best friends. She performed at so many of the events my parents attended, and was a family friend before I was even born. When Mum went away, Ellie said goodbye to her career, and took over as the 'woman' in my life. She'd chosen a career as a performing pianist

169

over having children, and had realised too late that she would have liked both. Ellie was a natural mother. She was so kind. And more importantly, she never left my side. Ellie worked seven days a week, and refused to have time off.'

'She sounds like she was really dedicated.'

'Yeah, she was. 'You'd have loved listening to her play.'

'I'm sure I would have.'

They sat down on the sofa, tea on the table in front of them, looking out to sea. Their bare bodies tangled over each other.

'She couldn't let go of playing piano entirely, of course, and in bed at night I'd hear her playing. I'd come down in my pyjamas,' he said, remembering everything in great detail, 'sitting at the bottom of our huge staircase, and she'd see me out of the corner of her eye and start playing children's tunes. It was amazing! Every night I'd creep back down the stairs, after she'd tucked me into bed, and say "Play for me!", and of course, she would.'

Sequoia smiled, her hand on his.

'That's why you were so desperate for me to play?'

'Yeah. Ellie was one of the few truly great things about my childhood.'

'If I'd known, honey; if I'd known, I would never have resisted. I would have understood. Really.'

'You didn't need the weight of my past on your shoulders. You had your own grief. And I knew if I told you that you'd take it on as if it was your own, and that wouldn't have been fair.'

'You wanted to protect me?'

'From the very moment I laid my eyes on you!'

Sequoia moved in to Ruben's house that day, and as each day passed she discovered that it was true: she'd never been far from his thoughts during the past eight years. His development company, S. Hazelwood, was actually listed in all legal documents as Sequoia Hazelwood Incorporated. She traced his movements through the missing eight years via newspaper articles, magazine features about the company, passport stamps, the rolling out of *Sequoia Royale* Hotels worldwide, and countless awards for design excellence.

Sequoia's eight years had been spent quietly, cooking her way through life. Cooking, baking, nurturing, as had been in her lineage. Now their worlds had come together. And day by day, Ruben pulled back from his work load and spent time devoted to his relationship. Even though he still designed ecologically sound architecture, Ruben no longer felt the need to build hotels. His mission had been accomplished.

Sequoia worked at *Treble Clef* a couple of days each week until near the end of pregnancy, but then passed it over to Ali for good.

Dozens of men continued to come forward, each wanting to claim Ruben's rich reward for finding the "Sequoia National Park Love Child". They'd all been convinced they were her father. It made for many amusing conversations between Sequoia and her dad. They both knew that her mum only ever had eyes for one man.

Ruben and Sequoia both fell in love again when their baby was born peacefully in the middle of Summer, beneath a waxing Moon which lit up the whole of Coles Bay. A gorgeous daughter transformed their lives, and gave every day a new purpose.

A Year and a Half Later

'You want *what*?' Ruben laughed out loud, running his fingers through his hair, incredulous at his fiancé's request.

'You heard me, Mr Hazelwood. I want two weddings.'

'The Queen of Minimalism wants *two* weddings?'

'Well you did say I could have anything I want, and that's what I want. Are you reneging on your pillow-talk promise, Mister?'

'If you want two weddings, then that's what you shall have. But why two?' he asked, shaking his head.

'I want the wedding that you want; the wedding that you expect with all the world's finest china and foods so expensive that you die of starvation because there's nothing on the plate,' she laughed wickedly, enjoying how easy it was to mock the lifestyles of the rich and famous. 'And I want the wedding that I dream of: a simple affair with so much food you can't eat for a week.'

'I think we can manage that,' Ruben smiled, walking closer to Sequoia. He reached out his hands, and picked up their daughter, Lisette. When she drooled down his expensive business suit it didn't bother him in the slightest. Everything was just so. Everything was as it should be.

'So, little miss, you need to help your mother sort out a couple of wedding dates.' Ruben looked at Sequoia and said, 'I've arranged a dress designer to come by this afternoon, and she can make you anything you want. There are no limits, okay? The Hotel can handle the catering, dependent on your choices and approval. And we can have the reception in the ballroom. Is that okay with you?'

'Honey, as I said, you can have *anything* you want for your wedding,' she winked, 'and so long as you're there I couldn't be happier.'

'Just one thing: let's do this soon. I don't want to wait any longer,' Ruben said impatiently.

'I think we should probably just have one honeymoon though. I don't want to be greedy,' she said seriously, tossing her long hair back over her shoulders. And then her laughter peeled through the room. 'I'm only joking. I don't want two honeymoons.'

'You *could* have two honeymoons though. If you wanted,' he assured her. 'And where do you want to go for our honeymoon, my love? Take your pick of hotels anywhere in the world' he said, gesturing wide. 'I could probably recommend one or two suitable for a princess such as yourself.'

'Actually,' she said hesitantly, not quite sure how to play this and most definitely not wanting to offend him: 'I don't want to stay in one of our hotels.'

'Why does that not surprise me?' he chuckled. 'I suppose you want to sleep in a tent?'

'If you're in it, then yes! If you plan to ravish me the whole time, then heck yeah, give me a tent!'

'And do you care where this tent is?' he laughed, moving his face from side to side as little Lisette pulled at his chin while he blew kisses on her soft rosy cheek.

'Okay, I'm happy to have a more comfortable bed for my honeymoon lovemaking. I don't *really* want to go camping,' she admitted. 'But I do want to go to Napa Valley and meet my family. All of them!' she said excitedly, her arms spread wide as if she were containing the whole family.

'I want to get to know that side of my family. I can't make up for all the lost years, but I can at least spend some time there.'

Ruben's face darkened. 'And when exactly would we enjoy our honeymoon? I can hardly ravish you in front of your grandparents and cousins.'

'I'm sure we'll manage!' they laughed together.

Lisette
invites you to the wedding of her parents
Sequoia Lissen and Ruben Hazelwood
April 30th at 4pm,
At the chapel in the vineyard,
Freycinet, Coles Bay

Followed by a
Reception in the ballroom
at Hazelwood Hotel, Coles Bay, Tasmania, Australia.
Black Tie

Scott Mitchell's new vineyard was adjacent to Tasmania's famed Freycinet National Park. Sequoia had delighted in his personal tour, observing traditional techniques of barrel fermentation and maturation. Scott explained how tight-grain French oak casks meant minimal intervention to ensure the wines retain their maximum colour and flavour.

Today, however, her thoughts weren't on wine or wine barrels or grape vines, but her wedding to Ruben Hazelwood. The man she'd waited a decade to marry. The man she loved with every beat of her heart. The man who caused her to keep breathing. *The father of her child*. The man who brought her own father back into her life.

As she walked in through the wooden front doors of the old sandstone chapel in the vineyard, she was taken aback at the jam-packed congregation. Every pew was full, and more than a hundred smiling faces were looking up at her. In that moment, her heart couldn't have been happier. All this love around her; around *them*. This is what community feels like, she thought, and although she'd spent eight years creating that for herself, somehow seeing everyone together made it feel more real. This was her home.

A string quartet of two violins, a viola and a cello bowed Pachelbel's *Canon in D*. Her steps were soft as she walked up the red carpet, careful to make eye contact with as many people as possible, all the time knowing that Ruben was only looking at one person: her.

Autumn sunshine poured through the stained-glass windows, and the myriad colours reflected off her dress. Sequoia had worked daily with the dress designer to create a vintage-inspired gown. Short, capped sleeves of embroidery sat snugly over her shoulders. The dress was coral and gold, with fitted cups moulded over her ample breasts, and loosely fitted around her curvaceous, child-bearing hips. It flowed down spilling over at her feet as if like a succession of waves lapping on the shoreline.

A beaded gold veil, to shoulder length, shrouded her face in the sheerest way possible. Beneath it, she wore her hair up high, with loose wisps hanging near her cheekbones, but not low enough to hide her dimples. Upon her feet were gold slippers with the faintest of heels. She considered Ruben was lucky that she was wearing shoes at all. And so did he! More than once, he told her how grateful he was for the compromises she made for this wedding day. What he didn't know, was that nothing, nothing at all, would have been too much bother for her as she and Lisette became Hazelwoods.

Ali and Mihan were chosen as bridesmaids, and they followed her up the aisle, each wearing soft gold dresses in a simple 1920s style in keeping with the vintage theme.

Fittingly, Max was the best man, and Alexander, the page boy. Sequoia couldn't help an empathic smile at the boy's freshly grazed face. The whole left side was red, raw, and only just beginning to form scabs to knit the broken skin. He'd fallen off his bike just yesterday, and was worried he'd be ousted from the wedding party.

'No chance at all,' Sequoia promised him. 'We want you there, even with that beautiful bleeding cheek. Our wedding wouldn't be the same without it.' In a short time, she had truly come to love Alexander.

As Sequoia came to stand in front of Ruben, he lifted her veil, and kissed her tear-soaked cheek.

'Stunning. Absolutely stunning.'

'You don't look too bad yourself, Mister,' she smiled. 'I can't believe I'm standing here. Tell me this is real. Pinch me.'

'Later,' he winked.

The ceremony drew on old traditions, with an emphasis on readings, music and thoughts on love and marriage which were personal to both of them.

Photos in the vineyard were taken against the backdrop of the Sun setting over the vines. *The harvest*, she smiled to herself. *The rich rewards, at long last.*

The wedding menu banquet was mouthwatering, and Sequoia felt she probably couldn't have done a better job if she'd slaved away in the kitchen all week. It told the story of their life and love.

Courgette and tarragon soup with lime creme fraiche: a favourite soup Sequoia's mother made each year when the tarragon in their garden invaded all the other herbs. The other option:

Tuscan white-bean soup, served with parmesan croutons to remind her of the moment she knew that Ruben wanted to marry her, and their glorious evenings in the thermal pool; and supper on the balcony at sunset.

Wild mushroom and red pepper stroganoff, served in a puff-pastry case and topped with deep-fried battered onions and a creamy red-wine sauce. This was an imitation of the first meal she'd ever eaten in Scotland, when they stayed at Ruben's Highland castle. It had been served on fine china and with silver service, but within minutes Sequoia had Ruben camped out on the rug by the huge open fireplace. Ruben was so dazzled by her laughter that he'd forgotten every form of etiquette which had been drummed into him from the day he was born. The castle staff were bewildered, but Ruben was enchanted.

Stack of eggplant fritters and beef tomato and potato discs topped with fried leeks and served with a spicy yoghurt sauce. A Parisian specialty she'd eaten late one Sunday afternoon. Ruben had taken her on a tour of designer boutiques, and they ran into the nearest café to get out of a hailstorm. They were famished, and devoured every morsel.

Welsh Glamorgan sausages on a bed of crushed-coriander mashed potato, served with a creamy peppercorn sauce. This was to honour Ruben's mother's Welsh origins.

Classic Italian rotolo with fresh asparagus, courgette and red peppers in a roll of garlic potatoes and pastry served with a creamy red pepper and white wine sauce. Sequoia had eaten this at Ruben's favourite restaurant in Tuscany. They'd been carried away walking all day, laughing, talking and making love, and there was nowhere to eat but a tiny eatery he knew of which was tucked away in the back streets. He swore he'd never eaten there before, and pretended it was a surprise find, but Sequoia couldn't help marvel at how a tiny restaurant, with seating for just eight, could rustle up a meal like this at midnight. It was clearly patronised by the rich. The *very* rich.

Baked beef tomato filled with couscous, pine nuts, sweet corn and served with a watercress sauce. This was chosen because her father Scott loved couscous, and asked her to make it each time he came for dinner.

Chocolate truffle torte with brandy and biscuit base served with chocolate shards and vanilla crème. Despite its richness, and against all sensible dietary odds, this had eased her morning sickness, so she knew it was a good-luck charm!

Champagne, lavender and lemon syllabub with berries and millionaire's shortbread. The first time Sequoia ever sipped champagne was on the night she went to Ruben's penthouse in Paris, and he'd opened her up to being a woman. She'd no idea that it cost six hundred euros a bottle; not until she'd asked Ruben for the name of it so she could use it in this recipe. *Ouch,* was all she had to say.

As Sequoia watched the guests, seated in the large dining hall with its twin log fire-places, oak panelling and magnificent staircase, she hoped it was all Ruben had dreamed of for their wedding.

Ruben's wedding gift to her was a secret. When they got up to start their bridal dance, a singer emerged

178

from the side of the stage. He'd flown Nora Jones in for a special performance. Her soulful voice sang *Turn Me On*. Sequoia couldn't contain her tears, and even managed to join her later for a duet.

The whole evening, they danced the night away, then stayed in the honeymoon suite. Ruben had brought a piano in, so she could play for him. Sequoia played on the piano for him alright, but in a completely new way. The top of that baby grand had never experienced anything like that in its life, and probably never would again!

Tomorrow, they'd be en route to their second wedding.

Sequoia emerged from the canopy of flowering cherry trees, the soft, baby-pink tear-shaped petals like confetti under her bare feet. For her second wedding, she wore a simple empire-line dress, in ivory chiffon and lace, that she'd sewn herself whenever Lisette slept.

Ruben had honoured her wish: a simple wedding, in her hometown village in rural France where they first met, surrounded by just a handful of friends and family. Sequoia said it would help her to feel like her mother was there, watching over her.

The ceremony, led by the village priest, was held outdoors near the river. The townsfolk gathered around, enchanted by how their 'girl' had blossomed.

Although Ruben's parents had flown over to Australia for the wedding, they also attended here, bringing tears to Sequoia's eyes for she'd expected they'd decline such a 'common' event. They would never again attend a wedding like this in their life, she was sure of that: a wedding that had a reception on picnic rugs by the river, the church bells chiming in the background, children running around with glee. No, she was certain that they'd never attend a wedding where the guests brought their favourite meals to share in lieu of gifts!

Sequoia's long wavy hair hung loose, and was now as long as the length of her back. From the first day she saw Ruben in Coles Bay, she let it grow again. It was the day she realised that she wasn't running anymore.

In her hands was a simple posy of Renaissance-blue cornflowers, and a matching garland woven into her hair.

Sequoia came into view from beyond the floral pink covering, as if it were curtains on a stage, and she the lead actress. A hushed silence preceded the soulful string sounds of a solo cello. Scott beamed as he led her forward.

Ruben, holding their beautiful daughter, Lisette, was standing under an oak tree, wearing the ivory linen slacks, rolled up to three quarter length, and the open-necked loose, long-sleeved shirt, she'd sown. Sequoia smiled even more when she saw his feet were bare on the mossy grass.

Arm in arm with her father, she walked forward. Her history, her future: worlds colliding. Tears slipped down her cheeks. It was okay. Ruben would brush them away.

But when Scott Mitchell looked over at his daughter, he knew it was his job. Catching teardrops in his hand, he whispered 'Your mother would have been so proud of you,' he croaked, his voice shaking. 'So proud. I have never been happier in my life than I am right at this moment.'

The cellist's strings played out the tune of *The Wedding Song*.

Struggling to contain her emotions, Sequoia took one simple step at a time. Although she'd already married the love of her life in Tasmania, in the opulence that the Hazelwood dynasty expected, and oh how she'd loved every moment of playing princess for a day, this wedding was different.

Today she was here in her hometown, where she and Ruben first met. Yes, it was the place where her heart had been ripped apart in the narrow cobble streets; but today was proof that the heart can survive. As the years rolled by, this date would mark the anniversary of her heart.

As Sequoia arrived at Ruben's side, she whispered 'Happy birthday, Ruben.'

Lisette reached out for her mama, her face bright and ecstatic.

'Mama,' she giggled, and wriggled from her father's hands to join her mother.

Lisette sat upon Sequoia's hip, reaching for the small cornflowers in her hair.

Ruben leant over and whispered to his feisty fairy, 'Eight years in exile was worth every minute just to see you walk through those trees to me. You are beautiful. And,' he said, tears sliding down his face, 'I love you.'

~ The End ~

Novels by Veronika Robinson

Mosaic
Bluey's Cafe

The Gypsy Moon Trilogy
Sisters of the Silver Moon
Behind Closed Doors
Flowers in Her Hair

Sweet Cinnamon Romance
Love at the Treble Clef Café
Love in a Scottish Storm
On the Wings of Love
Recipe for Love
House of Hearts

Moonlight and Motif
(*magical realism novels publishing in 2023*)
The Button Tin
The Soapmaker
The Irish Dollmaker

For a list of the author's non-fiction titles, visit
www.veronikarobinson.com

About the Artist: Heidi Harbers

Happiest when she's brightening up the world, whether it's decorating a room, painting a mural, growing a garden, feeding her chickens avocados, or organising fun events in her village, creativity is at the heart of Heidi's life.

As a pub landlady, and former restaurant owner, she has cooked for thousands of people across the years, serving up delicious meals, both traditional and unusual. When not cooking, Heidi's flare for transforming bare walls into canvases for her community to enjoy has earned her a wonderful reputation.

Australian born and raised, Heidi has travelled the world; and for many years has called England home. Born under the zodiac sign of Libra, the lovers, it is only natural that her art has found a home on the covers of romance novels.

Review Me

I hope you enjoyed reading
Love At The Treble Clef Café.

As an indie author, I'd be most grateful
if you could review this book on Amazon
or any other online book-reading platform.

I wish you a beautiful life.

www.ingramcontent.com/pod-product-compliance
Lightning Source LLC
Chambersburg PA
CBHW011521170626
46810CB00010B/3434